# FANTASIES OF A SUBMISSIVE

by

ROSALEEN YOUNG

CHIMERA

Fantasies of a Young Submissive first published in 2003 by
Chimera Publishing Ltd
PO Box 152
Waterlooville
Hants
PO8 9FS

Printed and bound in Great Britain by
Cox & Wyman Ltd, Reading.

This book is sold subject to the condition that it shall not, by way of trade or otherwise, be lent, resold, hired out or otherwise circulated without the publisher's prior written consent in any form of binding or cover other than that in which it is published, and without a similar condition being imposed on the subsequent purchaser.

The characters and situations in this book are entirely imaginary and bear no relation to any real person or actual happening.

### Copyright © Rosaleen Young

The right of Rosaleen Young to be identified as author of this book has been asserted in accordance with section 77 and 78 of the Copyrights Designs and Patents Act 1988

# FANTASIES OF A YOUNG SUBMISSIVE

Rosaleen Young

This novel is fiction – in real life practice safe sex

*This book is dedicated to the one to whom I owe my life and my soul,
N.B.*

*And to my beloved parents, who I pray will never read it.*

# Contents

| | |
|---|---|
| Index of Images | 6 |
| Foreword – about this book and its authoress | 7 |
| Vanity | 19 |
| The Woods | 28 |
| Eden | 41 |
| After the Ball | 43 |
| The Task | 58 |
| The Watcher | 68 |
| For a Mistress | 83 |
| Consequences | 85 |
| The Marionette | 119 |
| Worship | 133 |
| Lolita | 147 |
| Redemption | 149 |
| Libertinage | 163 |
| Arachne's Lair | 181 |
| Two Women | 187 |
| Her Majesty's Obsession | 189 |
| Emergence | 206 |
| Virgin | 216 |
| Afterword | 218 |

# Index of Images

*I wish to send a special thank you to the extremely talented and renowned photographic artist, Mike Crawley, for helping me to create the images in this book. It was extremely important to me that the imagery reflected the dark eroticism of the stories, and I couldn't have been more delighted with the result. I have appeared in thousands of photographs but within the pages here you will find some of the loveliest pictures ever taken of me.*

| | |
|---|---:|
| *Property* | Front Cover |
| *Homework* | 18 |
| *Forbidden Fruit* | 40 |
| *Captured Innocence* | 67 |
| *Bedtime* | 84 |
| *Resignation* | 118 |
| *Lolita* | 148 |
| *Freud's Vision* | 180 |
| *For the Taking* | 188 |
| *Restricted Pride* | 205 |
| *The Summer Harvest* | 215 |
| *Daydream* | 217 |
| *In Humble Servitude* | Back Cover |

# Foreword
## About this book and its authoress

Scratching the Surface

My name, as you have probably gleaned from the cover of this book, is Rosaleen Young. I am, as far as we are defined by what we do for a living, a Fine Art and fetish model. You may have seen my image on the cover of other books, in calendars or posters, in art exhibitions or on one of the fetish art websites on the Internet. More importantly, I am a lifestyle submissive and it is by that role that I prefer to express who I am.

I first began fetish modelling about a year ago. I was growing tired of my dull career in teen fashion and was aching for something more imaginative. Despite my own feelings of submission, I was ignorant to the fact that there were so many websites out there dedicated to my passions. It was only when I started to explore the Web that I truly found my niche. Fetish modelling fitted like a glove and gave me the opportunity to explore my submission and share the joy of it with others.

Modelling is, by its very nature, superficial. The girl is silenced, stripped of any personality and transformed into a face on a page. My writing helps me to claim back my voice and allow those who are interested to know a little of who I am beyond the green eyes and dark hair on the surface.

# The Young Submissive Female – A Self Analysis

The world of the submissive is filled with paradox. Through slavery I achieve freedom. I derive pleasure from my pain, power from my submission. The sensual excitement that I receive from being punished does not end at the physical level. I feel a deep psychological strength, relief, even pride at having endured it. I have tried to analyse my own feelings in order to derive some kind of psychological explanation for the way I am. I know that I am physically aroused by the sensation of pain on certain areas of my body but it is the mental rewards that are most important in understanding why I crave such sensations.

I am certain that a strict upbringing is a contributing factor. Although there was nothing sexual in the corporal punishment I received from my parents, the fact that someone loved me, was giving me attention and cared enough about my behaviour to take such measures to correct it was a genuine comfort. A sense of relief follows, a feeling of having paid for my crimes and been washed clean again. There is also a tremendous sense of relief in submitting completely to the will of another. All thoughts and responsibilities are lifted from my shoulders and I can relax in the knowledge that I am in safe hands.

Growing up in a conservative, Presbyterian family, I was made to feel guilty over the slightest inappropriate thought let alone having naughty fantasies about being dominated and punished. In an endless and ironic cycle, I found myself chastised for these feelings by the very subject that they were centred around – being spanked.

I have often been asked what it means to be a true submissive. There is no generic answer to this question.

Submission is expressed in different ways in different people. There are those who like to adhere to the many clichés they read about in books, the wearing of a collar, the removal of any underwear, the lowering of the eyes. For others these elements may or may not come into play. It is up to each couple to decide the pattern of behaviour that is right for them and how they wish to explore the dominant and submissive aspects of their relationship. To me, submission is an expression of love. As such it is no different than the act of marriage, the collar (be it physical or psychological) holds the same symbolism as the wedding ring. The submissive, like the bride in traditional ceremonies, promises her complete obedience, body and the entirety of her love to one Master or Mistress. Sometimes the owner may choose to lend her to others for a time. Sometimes the owner allows no one else to touch her. Either way she has chosen to sacrifice her will out of love, perhaps the most selfless of all expressions of love.

I am still far from fully understanding this socially forbidden yet powerful key to my sexual self. That is why I have chosen to explore my own fantasies through writing erotica. Each story is conjured from the depths of my imagination and from my experiences in my own world of submission and slavery.

Early Beginnings

I don't know exactly when it was that I first realised I had feelings of submission. Three incidences stand out in my memory as flagging up such tendencies even during my early childhood.

I remember that, at about the age of five, I was given a

small picture book of nursery rhymes. In the middle of the book was the story of the Queen-of-Hearts (who made some tarts, etc). The rhyme progressed, as you may recall, telling of the King-of-Hearts beating the knave full sore for stealing the Queen's tarts. Beneath the writing was a cartoon drawing of the King sitting atop his throne with the Knave pulled sorrowfully over his knee. He was wailing as the King's stern hand descended on his posterior in chastisement. Somehow that simple, innocent image (and particularly the plight of the Knave) seemed to strike a chord with me, so much so that I carefully traced the picture with my crayons – my first piece of spanking porn! I remember how red-faced I became when my father entered the room to look at what I had been drawing, though I did not understand why I felt ashamed.

When I was older I used to entertain myself with mind movies about all sorts of painful things happening to my bottom. Silly, childish things back then – being caned by a stern headmistress in a Victorian schoolroom for rudeness in class, having my buttocks stung by a swarm of angry bees for attempting to take their honey, or being paddled for stealing apples from a farmer's orchard. In every scenario I was the helpless victim of my superiors and was punished accordingly. I would sometimes pinch my buttocks as I played these fantasies in my mind, and very occasionally raided my mother's sewing kit to find a couple of sharp needles to prick myself with as well. Though I did not touch my genitals (that area was forbidden and its possibilities had not yet entered my chaste, Christian-girl's mind) I knew that these thoughts and the stinging sensations I produced in my bottom gave me a feeling of extreme pleasure – warm, happy, naughty.

I was spanked for naughty behaviour countless times

and had even endured several tastes of the wooden spoon, but these incidents were always purely for punishment. They held no kind of sexual gratification, being always delivered by my parents. My mind movies were no longer enough to keep me satisfied. My curiosity of what the sensation of a real, erotic spanking might be like could no longer be restrained. I locked myself in my bedroom and retreated to the sanctuary of my wardrobe. Inside the wardrobe was my little cubby-hole, my secret place containing a blanket, a lamp, a few books and my emergency stash of chocolate (for when I was sent to my room). Taking a wooden coat hanger I began to spank my bottom repeatedly, drinking in the sensation that awoke in my virgin flesh. At first the pain was unbearable and I felt I could not go on but then, as the burning diffused and spread through me, I began to crave more. I did not stop until my buttocks were black and blue with bruises.

The act reduced me to tears, not because of the pain in my buttocks but the overwhelming shame I felt at enjoying it. I believed myself to be a freak of nature, completely alone in my bizarre perversion. I knew nothing of the flagellant monks who practiced similar rituals regularly with knotted whips, cleansing themselves of sin. Nor was I aware of the masses of literature dating back through the centuries that revealed a masochistic nature in man. I knew nothing of DeSade or Sacher-Masoch or of their contemporaries, which exist in the form of spanking magazines and BDSM novels, nor did I know of the thousands of Internet sites devoted to my tastes. It was not until several years later that I began to discover these things and felt the glorious relief of safety in numbers.

As my sexual feelings began to mature I developed many richer, darker fantasies than the simple spanking scenarios

I mentioned, though they still play a major part in what turns me on. My desires delved into a need for submission and to serve a Master or Mistress. I wanted to belong to them, to be theirs in total devotion – their property, their slave. Books like *Story of O* by Pauline Reage helped me to better understand my own nature, but only to a degree. I am still learning. Unlike many who experiment with or live the dominant/submissive lifestyle, I have never felt any desire to 'switch' and adopt the dominant role. I have always felt pure submissiveness. It is the core of my sexual and psychological self.

On Terminology

Submissive. Slave. Masochist. Pain-girl. Bottom. I have often heard such terms passed around the smoky, rubber-choked Fetish clubs of London and in Internet chatrooms that cater to 'friends of BDSM'. But what do the words really mean? What am I exactly? I feel that we can become bogged down in technicalities and labels so I greet terms like these with one eyebrow raised and use them extremely loosely. To be honest, I find the very concept of 'sadomasochism' rather ridiculous and the word has developed negative connotations. Freud believed that sadism and masochism were one and the same thing (masochism being sadism turned inwards towards the self rather than outwards towards the world) and postulated the idea of a sadomasochistic personality, which comprises elements of both. This concept, like many of Freud's ideas, has filtered into society and contributed to ignorance and condemnation. In my experience in the industry, I have met people who could certainly be described as masochists but very few sadists. The

'Masters' and 'Mistresses' brandishing whips and leading their 'slaves' around at fetish clubs cannot be seen as sadistic. Such relationships are based on the mutual respect of the partner's limits. Logically speaking, a person who is actually sadistic could never form a satisfactory relationship with a masochist because the very nature of true sadism relies on the victim's lack of pleasure from their pain or humiliation (which the masochist obviously thrives upon).

On Social Acceptance

Part of the purpose of this book is to send a message to any likeminded people out there. People who, like me, burn with desires that need to be satisfied but who find they wrestle with society and with themselves over them, still caught as we are under the thumb of Victorian morality – curious men and women who have, perhaps, bought this book in a flustered hurry, shoving it carefully under a pile of 'normal' publications and making certain that they did not catch the bookseller's eye.

The range of fantasies that, shall we say, stray from the accepted norm is infinite. Although there is a certain degree of overlap, every individual's fantasies and fetishes are specific to them. Yet society ties them all clumsily and ignorantly under the same BDSM umbrella. To many, those who would rather judge than venture towards an understanding, the emphasis in 'sadomasochism' is on sad! Masochism features in the Diagnostic and Statistical Manual of Mental Disorders. The Oxford Dictionary categorises masochism as 'a form of sexual perversion'. Perversion – that anvil-weighted word which lumps masochism in with Paedophilia or Bestiality! All else dissolves so that it is this label that society sees and not the person or their acts. Even the concept of fetishism seems to be one that society shuns, but as fetishism is technically the admiration of an inanimate object or body part, surely all the thousands of self-proclaimed 'normal' men who buy a newspaper every morning to ogle at the enormous chest of the latest page three model could be considered 'breast fetishists'.

The two most important words to bear in mind when passing judgement over what is moral and what is not must surely be 'consenting adults'. If two adults are both willing to explore their sexuality without bringing harm to anyone, what right has a stranger to decide what is an appropriate course for their sex life to take?

The situation for the masochistic female is arguably worse. Until very recently, women have been largely denied the right to have sexual fantasies. Pornographic literature and art has, for centuries, catered to male sexual needs whilst, ironically, the beauties that inspired such novels, drawings, paintings and photographs were not expected to entertain erotic thoughts themselves. The equal status women have sought to achieve is equality in all aspects of life – in business, in politics and also in sexuality. As with the first two, advancement in sexual equality is progressing very slowly. The world of exotic dancing is a good example. Films like *The Full Monty* make it acceptable, even comical, for a man to pursue a career in this industry. Now compare that to something like *Showgirls*, which portrays the world of female exotic dance as sleazy and dirty. Similarly with sexual fantasies, it is still far more shocking and unacceptable for a woman to come right out and say, 'Hey, I'm into spanking!' than for a man to do the same.

The feminist movement tends to frown at the submissive female believing that, in her choosing a life of servitude (returning to the bedroom and chaining herself there), she is idly throwing away the liberties and equalities that women have worked towards for so many years. I take nothing away from those struggles. What they have provided the modern woman with is a choice. She can live as an equal or to dominate if she wishes. But she may also make the decision to remain a slave. Through her choice, her situation differs greatly from the enforced slavery of women that we have seen in the past.

At this stage in my life I am still in school-mentality, wishing to fit in and insecure about what others will think of me and of my tastes. I am happy revealing my desires to likeminded people but still uncomfortable about 'coming out' to the rest of society. I am told that as one grows older one cares less and less about others' opinions. It therefore saddens me to hear stories from middle-aged men or women who have spent years hiding their particular fantasy from their partner out of shame or fear of judgement. Or, most distressing of all, they *have* mentioned it to their partner only to be met with panic, disgust or even rejection. It is not our right to judge but judge we do, harshly and without understanding. Most people fear what does not make sense to them and it is difficult to see the world through someone else's eyes, especially where sexual tastes are concerned. It is perhaps the naivety and idealism of my youth talking but I still believe that building an understanding of what our fantasies are and where they come from is the key to tolerance and eventually, acceptance.

I am reminded of a quote from one of my dearest friends and greatest inspirations, Lucy. Although still in her prime, she has worked as a prostitute, a pornographic model, a dominatrix and a madam and has done in her sexual life a multitude of things that society would deem as immoral. I will always remember her turning to me with her characteristic grin and asking, 'Do you know what the biggest regret of my life is?' I shrugged my shoulders sheepishly. 'That I didn't buy these shoes in white!'

On this book

I am a passionate girl and writing this book has provided me with a safe haven in which I can vent all the wild fantasies and sexual frustrations that come with being a virgin. Perhaps it is rather odd to be writing about things I have not yet experienced, but I see no reason why I can't run riot in my mind. Here I can go to all the places that I cannot go to in real life. Some of my fantasies are a little farfetched but what do I care? That is what fantasy is for, limited only by the imagination itself. Elements of each story are real as they reflect parts of me – my ideas and my experiences in my new career as a fetish model and life as a slave. I could not select a single story to represent my sexual interests as they evolve and fluctuate depending on my mood. My writing style also tends to change from story to story to reflect that mood and the many aspects of my sexuality. Sometimes, as I masturbate, I simply long for a sound spanking, something cliché and classic like being spanked in my school uniform over the knee of a strict headmaster. At other times I crave dark psychological submission and true enslavement that will challenge my own physical and mental boundaries. Every one of these fantasies arouses me in a different way and you can be sure that I had to take many pauses during the writing of my stories in order to slip into my bedroom and relieve the tension.

The fact that I choose to remain a virgin until I marry seems to fascinate a lot of people, which is why I am mentioning it here. I know it is a rare phenomenon in this day and age but my decision is largely due to my old-fashioned upbringing. Thankfully I am not a virgin through lack of offers, simply through lack of the right offers (or rather, offers from the right person). Sex to me is sacred. I believe that it is the most precious thing a slave has to give her master and also that a woman has to give a man. After all, the same symbolism exists between the metal band that is placed around a slave's neck and the metal band that is placed around a bride's finger. The person I give myself to will be everything to me – husband and master – for as long as I live.

In some ways staying steadfast in my decision gives me the chance to explore all kinds of other routes to sexual pleasure rather than diving into straightforward sexual intercourse. I have all this wonder yet to experience, but for now all my fantasies shall be channelled into words on a page. Thank you for sharing them with me.

*Homework*

# My Fantasies

# Vanity

*I have been shamefully conceited about my bottom for as long as I can remember. One of the reasons I went into modelling was that it gave me the chance to show off this feature, exposing its loveliness to the world. This story centres on a young girl's obsession with her bottom and, in particular, her longing for someone to spank it. I must admit that there is more than a tad of myself in its heroine.*

What care I if my passion for my mirror would make Narcissus himself blush with shame? What care I if I spend my time gazing for hour after hour at the loveliness reflected back at me? My mirror is my best friend. He constantly tells me that I am beautiful. He allows me to make detailed studies of my every feature as my body undergoes the transformation from budding girlhood to the bloom of a young woman.

My long, chestnut mane of hair forms a perfect frame around the elfin features of my face. My wide, emerald eyes give the illusion of childlike innocence but, if you gaze a little closer, you will see the rare and sparkling fire that betrays the mischievousness of my disposition. The petite delicacy of my nose and mouth is echoed in the rest of my body. My breasts, firm with youth, are proud and pert. My waist and limbs are toned and slim, and my back defiantly arched. But none of these features (although superb I have concluded) can compare to the sheer perfection of my favourite physical attribute. For my crowning glory is, without doubt, my magnificent bottom. Oh yes, surely it is the work of Aphrodite herself, made in the image of her own unsurpassable form! My buttocks hold a bewitching magic of their very own, drawing all eyes towards them with an almost magnetic force. The flawless curves sweep upwards to gently kiss each other in worship. The skin itself is like the finest velveteen. I could fondle and caress it for hours, and I do.

I admit that the excellence of my bottom has become something of an obsession to me. I am in the habit of meticulously examining every bottom that I chance upon – my girlfriends with whom I share a locker room at my school, elegant ladies unwittingly displaying their anatomical wares at the department store, tight-skirted waitresses at the fine restaurants that father sometimes takes me to. All those bottoms have fallen under my scrutiny. Hundreds of them, maybe thousands, and despite the exactness with which I peruse their curves, I have never seen a single one that even comes close to the perfection of my own. My rear view retains an air of enticing majesty, demanding the eye to devour with a ravenous appetite.

I have overheard others talk about me many times. My name is generally accompanied by words like 'conceited' and 'haughty'. I cannot deny that I am worthy of these descriptions, that I am the epitome of a spoilt brat. I like to get my own way and I throw a furious tantrum if I do not. I am also a frightful tease! As I watch my body's curves developing I can only imagine the effect they must have on the opposite sex. I spend hours trying on the generous selection of clothes that daddy-dear and mummy-dear have bought me. Please do not think they actually permit me to wear the skimpy attire I enjoy. But as soon as I am out of their sight I pull my blouse a trifle tighter and roll up my skirt so that it does justice to the treasure it hides.

Bending over in my taut panties, skimpy shorts, cheek-hugging trousers and painted-on skirts which would not pass as belts for a larger girl, I have turned the tantalisation of men into an ingenious art form. I am shameless! The pursuit of showing men what they cannot have is a never-ending source of delight for me, and I engage in it with military precision. The alluring way I wiggle my bottom as I walk or bend right over from the waist to tie a shoelace at an appropriately selected time, when an audience of ogling lads is nearby, is a testament to my expertise. They can gape and stare till their tongues scrape the ground. They can even whistle or make their Neanderthal-esque comments (usually no more imaginative than 'Gorgeous ass, love!'). I will simply let rip with a dismissive giggle or feign offence, pouting impudently. How seething with jealousy all the other women must be, to see how obviously their own bottoms pale in comparison to mine! I bet they wish they could shoot darts from their eyes to plunge into its supple flesh and blight its pure faultlessness.

Almost superstitiously I perform my private ritual every day behind the locked door of my bedroom. With the aid of the three carefully arranged mirrors I make detailed studies of myself in every angle and position. I stand erect and trace the mysterious valley between and beneath the twin-globes of my rump with my nimble fingertips. In this position the curvature of my buttocks resembles two bouncy beach balls side-by-side. I bend over further to watch the lower creases disappear and my whole posterior tilting upwards invitingly. Arching my limber spine, I stick out the object of my praise as I stand on tiptoe and double over to touch the floor. As my silken cheeks pucker against the stern, icy slate of the mirror, I feel the coldness biting into the naked flesh as if it were punishing me for my vanity.

The sensation awakens me. Peeking beneath the glorious hemispheres I can see the moisture glistening on my femininity. The very sight of my own voluptuous ass makes my flowering clitoris begin to crave attention. My skilfully practiced fingers dive between my legs and stroke amorously at my impatient rosebud. Falling on my bed, my mind still alive with fresh images of the sensuous nakedness of my rounded globes, I work greedily, tickling and tantalising myself to make the feeling escalate. My fingers saturate themselves in my slippery dew as I whimper under my own developing sexual prowess. My succulent fruit is ripening. My other parts melt away and I become all cunt.

Now, in the darkness behind my eyelids, is when it starts to happen. Images begin to flash across my mental picture theatre. The scenes differ from one to the next but the theme is always the same. My secret desire – spanking. I am into spanking. Into it in a big way. I long for it. My deepest wish is to be soundly spanked until my bottom turns red. It sounds so silly. I could never mention it to anyone. God, how embarrassing! But whenever I get steamy and my eyes close into fantasy, I see myself bent over and receiving the corporal punishment I long for. That must be why I am so fixated by my bottom. I like to make sure it is the most perfect spank-target in existence. I congratulate myself for having such bold fantasies at such a relatively young age. My girlfriends are all busy imagining that they are making love to Brad Pitt or Robbie Williams, but whilst I work my clitty, memories of every hand that has ever been raised in correction against my trembling bottom melt in and out of focus. I recall the day I dared to play truant and was turned smartly around and tilted at an angle to receive 'six of the best' with father's slipper. And the time, when my parents had gone out for the evening, that my babysitter pinned me down on the bed, pulled down my cotton pyjama-bottoms and let her flailing ruler teach me what happens to naughty girls who refuse to go to sleep.

Most potent of all my memories is that journey on the empty train carriage not two years ago. Certain that I would not be caught I had snuck onboard without paying my fare. When the inspector burst into the carriage and demanded my ticket, I not only failed to produce it but also made the added mistake of being impertinent. Perhaps he'd had a bad day and this incident was the last straw, or maybe he had a secret penchant for spanking girls' bottoms in the private world of secluded train carriages. I shall never know the true motivation for his unorthodox action. All I know is that he promptly sat himself down on the seat next to me and dragged me over his knee to deliver a few expertly-aimed slaps on the seat of my pleated skirt. I remember with distinct clarity the scorching sensation that grew in my unsuspecting flesh. He and I had seemed frozen in time as if we had been removed from the rest of the world. A rampage of confused emotions consumed me. There were the expected reactions of shame at being treated in such a childish manner and the obvious sting that his smacks injected through the thin material, but there was also something else, a primitive emotion that seemed to have been awakened from the depths of my being. I feared it and yet sought to prolong it. I could not understand why I felt a twinge of disappointment when his hand ceased its regular descent and he marched off into the next carriage.

Afterwards, as I sat with my warm bottom pressed into the seat, I could not get the experience out of my mind. Other passengers joined the carriage at the next stop, squashing into the seat opposite me. I shifted uncomfortably. The rigid seat evoked new prickling sensations in my tormented bottom and I whimpered audibly. I glanced around in embarrassment. I was certain that people were staring at me. I was sure that they somehow *knew*. Every businessman buried behind a copy of his daily broadsheet, every mother holding onto her mewling child and every tourist attempting to make sense of the Tube map knew I had been turned over a man's knee and had my bottom reddened. Perhaps my thoughts were written all over my face. I desperately tried to think of something else but all I could focus on was the image of me being pulled like a disobedient girl over that accursed lap. How dare he do such a thing to me? How dare he put me through that degradation? I thought of screaming harassment but knew that it would never be taken seriously. Every other form of attack would have been viewed as legitimate. If only I'd been threatened verbally. But a spanking! Spanking is a law unto itself and the inspector knew it. I could imagine the media coverage of such a case. I would become a laughing stock.

'But he hurt my pride, Your Honour!'

'Really, young lady, I thought you said it was your bottom.'

How could I face my friends at school?

I could feel my face growing redder as I thought about it, and I hung my head wishing I could hide completely. Finally the train pulled into my stop. I fought my way out of the carriage and raced down the platform, knocking several angry pedestrians out of my way as I ran, and I did not stop running until I reached the sanctuary of our front door.

I fumbled with the key and slammed the door firmly behind me. I caught sight of myself in the hall mirror. I looked a state! My face was indeed as ruby-red as it felt and my hair hung about it in a dishevelled manner. I dropped my bag on the floor and raced up to my room. I locked the door and walked up to the mirror. Slowly I twisted around and glanced back over my shoulder, staring at the curve my bottom created in the pleated skirt-line, then reaching down I grabbed the hem of it. By now the sting of the spanking had subsided a little, leaving my bottom tender. I felt every inch of the material against it as I slid it up to my waist.

And there it was! Lasting proof of what had been done to me. The telltale signs of the punishment were unmistakable. A pink glow peeked out from beneath the taut navy line of my panties. I pulled them down and saw that the patch of colour formed two large and blotchy circles covering my entire buttocks. I knew I should have been shocked and outraged at the sight but somehow I could not draw my eyes away from it.

I was too young to recognise that the feelings aroused in me were those of intense sexuality. I had no idea that the inspector's horrid, gnarly old face and broad but precise hands would, in the years to come, fuel my masturbation and send forth my juices from within. Though the actual experience lasted less than a minute, my imagination extends and colours the delicious scene so it can last for hours. Sometimes I change the scenario, thinking up lots of different roles for the two of us. I imagine he is the headmaster at my school who calls me into his office every afternoon and, seated in his large leather chair, forces me into that familiar position again. Sometimes he uses his bare hand, sometimes a belt or a ruler, but every time the result is the same – my beautiful derriere is left crimson and hot.

As these thoughts envelope my mind I can no longer bear the craving. I must feel this sensation again. My parents have gone to a midday concert and will not be back for hours. Without even bothering to dress, I fling open my bedroom door and race downstairs and out into our large secluded garden. The sun warms my nakedness and a moist film of perspiration begins to form, making my honey-hued skin glisten. My bare feet sink into the soft lawn. The trees rustle and whisper their secrets to me as I share mine with them. I run over to the shed, unlatch the door and go inside the musty space. Then after only a short time I spy what I'm looking for. Standing on tiptoe I take down my old wooden ping-pong paddle from the shelf, and having brushed away the dust and cobwebs I stand motionless for a short time, gazing at the implement in my petite hand, about to be reborn to a new purpose.

How I wish my unlikely hero were here with me now, his reproachful hands ready to strike my inviting target, this time totally bare. The sense of longing overwhelms me. Here I stand, filled with a girl's passions. Is no one out there willing to help me realise them? Where is the stern Master who will take me under his wing and over their knee? Like the peaches ripens in our orchard, my bottom is now ripe for the punishment but, alas, no one is there to witness it but the grass and the trees.

I skip over to my favourite old oak, the one I often lay

beneath to read my books. In a flash I am poised, my hand against the sturdy trunk for support. I thrust out my behind, welcoming the paddle's devoted attention, my finely cleft buttocks, as flawless as if they are moulded in wax, exposing their glorious beauty to the world. As if observing some ancient decreed custom, I bring the paddle down upon my beckoning flesh. The sharp sting runs through me, arousing my body as it did before. I close my eyes and concentrate on the sensation. I drink it in. My full lips part slightly as a moan escapes them. The air absorbs my cries. I feel truly alive under the spell of this forbidden pleasure. My bottom, the loveliest since the history of time, throbs and glows. The rest of my body dissolves and all I feel is the smarting across my buttocks. The paddling falls like a rain of scorpions, stabbing their stings into firm teenage flesh. I want it to last forever yet I can stand no more. I hurl the paddle upon the ground and nearly swoon at the lingering fire it has left. I fall to my knees and I frig my sex furiously, probing the tip of my finger in deeper from time to time to smear the wet dew over my heated skin. I envisage my punisher's outrage if he were to witness my naughty, sluttish behaviour. He would surely punish me then, make my bum-cheeks an even more lustrous red in the late summer sun, red to match that of the garden roses. My clitty burns. The entrance to my womb opens like the petals of a flower and my sweet nectar washes over my hands. My convulsions die down and I collapse in a heap of exhausted pleasure, mixed with guilt. Is it guilt for my behaviour? Is it guilt for my feelings? Could that be why the idea of enduring such discipline is so desirous to me? That, whilst I may cry scalding tears of pain, there is a dark, secret joy in knowing that I am getting no more than I truly deserve!

Slowly I return to the house and dress myself again, a long satin skirt to hide my shame. A girl cannot remain forever in the world of fantasy. Reality claims her once again but I still have hope that one day someone will allow the two worlds to meet.

# The Woods

*I have a great love for the legends of the ancient Greeks. They are passionate, melodramatic and filled with grand scale themes like sex, love, death, gore and metamorphosis. The story of Pan in particular has always held my fascination. Pan was the god of the woods, mountainside and music as well as that of shepherds and their flocks. He aided hunters in finding their prey but was shown little respect in return. He was thought to have a fearful temper, and woe betided any traveller who disturbed his rest whilst journeying through the woods alone. He had the power to overwhelm them with a deep sense of fear. In this capacity he lives on today in the word 'panic'. He was wild in nature, brimming with anarchic, animalistic lust; Freud's Id incarnate. He is said to have spent much of his time chasing after the various nymphs (divine spirits of the brooks, trees, pools, etc). Pan is most often associated with carnality and rape. It is in this context that he appears in my fantasy. I want to make it clear that I do not condone any form of sexual practice that does not involve consent. A desire does exist, however, in the minds of many women (especially submissive ones) to be taken roughly, with force and against one's will. This story marries my eternal love of the woods with my obsession with the legend of this lascivious god.*

The girl is unafraid to walk in the woods alone. The woods are her home. She has been coming here since she was a child, though it was not until recently that her parents had let her make the journey unaccompanied.

Her love for this place goes far beyond a simple enjoyment of their beauty and tranquillity. The forest is her secret place, dark and intimate, thick with a private magic. Here time has frozen and she can abandon herself to her imagination. She likes to make elaborate garlands from the woodland flowers and pretends to be a princess in a flowery crown. It is her place of escape, a refuge from the constant lectures from her mother and father. She loves the woodland area in all seasons. She sees the changing beauty of each one with the wonder of a child. In the summer the heavy canopy provides a cool sanctuary from the heat of the sun. In the autumn the trees turn dry and golden and the whole forest looks as if it were on fire. Then the leaves cover the path like a blanket, crunching beneath her thin shoes. In the winter the trees turn to skeletons of their former selves and the snow transforms the place into a palace of alabaster. But most of all she loves the springtime, when everything is reborn and new life sprouts from every burrow, nest and seed. The whole area, at this time, seems to be held under a kind of enchantment.

She knows she shouldn't have strayed from the path but the flowers looked so much more delicate, mysterious and alluring here, away from the heavy, ignorant tread of man. Once off the path it was as though some supernatural force had collected her and borne her away to this place. She has ventured deep into the wood's heart. It is a heart that beats. Her tanned legs are warm and weary from the walk. She allows herself to sit for a minute on the ground and leans back against one of the trees. Through the flimsy material of her blouse the rough foliage makes tiny indentations on the velveteen skin of her shoulder blades. Her body squirms as she feels the harsh bite of the bark. The two textures press against one another, smooth against rough. The grass beneath her still holds the morning's dew. She pulls her skirts up to her thighs to cool herself. Speckles of light filter through the heavy foliage above and fall like confetti over her skin. She watches them dance on her belly as the breeze rustles the leaves. She is well aware that she must head for home soon or her mother will begin to worry.

As she rests there against the tree, it occurs to her that she has not felt this tired in a long time. She can feel her limbs growing heavier as though they were sinking into the ground. Her eyes begin to close. She tries to keep them open but the lids refuse to lift themselves. Once deprived of sight the sounds of the forest fill her ears. The sounds are always there – the calls of the different birds, the whisper of the breeze as it gossips with each leaf, the buzz of the insects busy at their work – but now they seem so much clearer than before.

It begins so faintly at first that she thinks she has imagined it, but the sound gradually increases in volume and she knows she is not mistaken. It is music. Music unlike any she has ever heard before. The sound is smooth and hollow, rising above the other woodland noises. It rises and falls in a continuous motion like the rolling of waves on the shoreline. It is strange, even eerie, but so very beautiful! The ear cannot help but want to listen to it. Then suddenly the tune ceases. A pair of squirrels chatter at one another from a nearby tree.

She shakes her head, wondering if she has heard

anything at all.

Then it begins again, louder this time. If she didn't know any better she would say it comes from some sort of pipe. It is filled with trills and crescendos. Its mood is both joyous and sorrowful at the same time, seeming to contain within its notes the essence of life itself. All other thoughts dissolve from her brain and her only wish is to keep on hearing the sound.

She cannot tell from which direction the music comes. It seems to be all around her, in the air itself.

Silence once more, and when the tune stops she feels as though she's been kicked in the stomach. She listens with her whole body, willing it to begin again, and at last it does recommence.

She leaps to her feet. It's as though the music itself is breathing energy into her limbs. She begins to run. She does not know where she is going. The music calls to her instinct, driving her onwards. Beneath her feet the ground feels alive, as though each blade of grass tilts to push her forward as she touches it. Her desperation grows with every step. She has to follow the music. She has to find its source. She continues running, hoping she will eventually gauge its direction. She becomes increasingly frustrated, fearful that the sound will stop forever and she will never discover the mysterious maker of the music. The trees around her become a blur. Finally the sound grows louder still. She is certain it is directly in front of her. She races towards it. It fills her ears, building and building until it feels as though it is coming from within her as well as all around. It becomes deafening and she cannot bear it any longer. She falls to the ground, clasping her hands to her ears.

Silence!

Slowly she raises her head, and discovers she's in the middle of a small clearing surrounded by a circle of trees. Their tops are less dense than the others and a shaft of sunlight penetrates through them, bathing her in a golden light. She squints, blinking into the brightness, and out of the corner of her eye she spies something moving behind the trees. Turning her head she thinks she sees a flash of brown. Then perfect stillness. She tells herself it is more than likely a deer startled by her presence, but she cannot shake off the dread that is growing inside her.

He watches her from behind the thick trunk of a nearby tree. He has seen her many times before but always from a distance. He has never allowed himself to get so close to her. He has always been afraid she would run from him as Syrinx did back in the ancient times in Arcadia. She had thought herself clever to turn herself into a bed of reeds to escape him. But he had plucked each one from its stem and made them into a pipe. Thus he kept the nymph by his side forever.

This girl shares her exquisite beauty. Even now, as he looks at her, he sees his love reborn into a new body. From the moment he first saw her he was mesmerised. Every time she visited his woods he would follow her. He had waited until the time was right, when she was no longer a skinny and awkward child. He had watched as her hips and her chest began to grow plumper, developing the curves that mark the beginning of womanhood. He had waited as she ventured further and further into the woods, deeper into his home, and this time she has crossed the border between her world and his. She is in his territory now, and must abide by his laws.

He lifts the pipes to his lips and plays again, and the

gnarled, ancient tree in front of him creaks as it begins to stretch its time-scarred branches like one awakening from a long sleep. Life and movement flows into them. The branches reach out and twist around her waist, pulling her tight against the sturdy trunk. She screams in terror, uncertain as to what is happening to her. She fights the branches, trying to push them away with her hands but her efforts are useless. She is trapped. The tree's roots writhe up from the ground, tossing away the dirt and leaves that have buried them for so long. They coil around her ankles like serpents, prising her legs and her thighs apart and holding them in place. Other branches tug at her clothes, shredding the material, bursting the buttons of her blouse and ripping the skirt from her waist.

The branches now secure her shoulders, waist and ankles, and she can barely move. A thin branch winds over her cheek and forces itself into her mouth, stifling her cries. The music plays on. Leaves graze lightly over her pert, delicate breasts and then tickle the place between her legs.

He takes the reed pipes from his lips, and as the music stops the tree, no longer under the enchantment of the sound, becomes still once more. The woods become as silent as death. Not so much as the chirp of a bird disturbs the heavy air. The girl's wide green eyes wildly search all around her. Her heart races and her hair covers her face, dishevelled and wet with perspiration.

Crouching like a leopard and keeping out of her sight, he emerges from behind the tree. His weather-roughened hands reach out to brush the exposed flesh of her ankle. She screams at the touch but the sound thuds bluntly against the wooden branch between her teeth. She tries desperately to look downwards so she can catch sight of her captor, but the thick branch in her mouth obscures him from her. She feels coarse hands stroking the smooth skin of her calves. They delve upwards to her thighs. She hears him sniffing her flesh and feels his long, curved nails pressing into her.

Now he nears her secret place. It will not be long. She knows it. Her body stiffens and she desperately tries to close her thighs, to lock the gate and keep out the intruder. Her muscles strain against the bonds but the tree roots hold her securely.

At last the hands reach the intimate folds below her womb. Her body jerks as they touch her and she tries to arch her spine and tilt her pelvis backwards towards the tree's trunk so he cannot view his target. The harsh bark scratches at her soft buttocks. She hears a grunt of indignant rage and a high-pitched note sounds through the air. There is a rumbling from deep inside the tree. The roots pull her knees further apart and an extra branch pushes its way between her coccyx and the trunk so that she is forced to display her wares. She weeps with fear and shame, gasping for breath between her wrenching sobs. Probing fingers pinch the virginal lips of her sex and separate them to reveal the rouge flesh beneath. Her brow creases. It is the first time anyone has touched her in this place. She feels the breeze enter the mouth of her vagina. Its coolness mingles with the humid warmth inside. She feels her captor's nose press dangerously close to her and hears a series of sharp sniffs like those made by a hound on the trail of a fox. She is powerless to prevent this violation. He grunts again, his nostrils flaring as he inhales her scent. The sound is deep, guttural and brimming with pleasure. The hands reach up to her breasts, gripping them gently, feeling their contours. He cups his hands under each as if measuring its weight. His fingers circle her nipples. He raises his head and she can feel the heat of his breath upon them. Her own breath comes in the shallow pants of sheer horror.

Finally he rises so that his face is directly in front of hers. Her eyesight is hazy with the tears, and frantically she blinks them away. All she can see is a pair of eyes. They stare back at her. They are almond-shaped and the same shade of green as her own. There is something strange about them that she cannot quite place, something unearthly. His pupils are the most bizarre she has ever seen, not round circles as they should be but thin, vertical ovals like those of a goat. Somehow, with the sight of his eyes, her panic drops away from her. It is as though she is forced into calmness. She wants to look away, to see the rest of his body, but she cannot take her eyes off his. They bind her to him. He has dreamed long about possessing her. It is not merely a part of his body that takes animal form. His mind, too, retains an air of primitiveness, of lust and greed without inhibition. It is his animal part that drives his loins and desire. The two parts of his mind are eternally in conflict – human against animal, kindness against savagery.

For a moment he simply looks at her, taking in the beauty of her face. Logic is pushed to the back of her brain. She knows she should be afraid. She knows she is helpless. She knows what he is intending to do with her. Yet his eyes are like comforting streams washing over her, washing her fear away. It is as though she is caught in a kind of trance. She no longer has control of her body. All she can do is watch, as he possesses it.

She feels his legs, thick with hair. She feels his sex against her, its hardness rising to push through the thin forest of her pubic hair. His body dips so that its tip rests at the entrance to her womb. She can feel the gigantic muscle as it pulsates against her, about to stretch open her coy, untarnished sex. She knows she should resist but it is not only her physical restriction that prevents her from doing so. She braces herself, biting down on the branch between her teeth. Her eyes remain wide and fixed on his.

Slowly he begins to push upwards. The tunnel of her womb opens as his hugeness forces it apart. She screams into the branch, the wood muffling the sound. Tears flood her eyes, blurring her vision. The hypnotic effect he's had over her melts away now she cannot see his eyes. Panic overwhelms her once more. She struggles against the branches, the bark chafing her flesh. He continues to thrust into her, grunting and snorting as he does so. The sharpness of the pain transforms to a dull throbbing. Gradually her vagina stretches to accommodate him. His robust hands rip away the branch from her mouth and he presses his lips to hers, but she shakes him off violently and lowers her head. She blinks the tears away. As her vision clears she can see a large pair of cloven hoofs like those of a goat next to her own bare feet.

Her gaze moves upwards, over the tawny, fur-lined legs, over the muscular, human skin of the waist and chest to the face in front of hers. Careful not to look directly into his eyes she takes in the whole form of the head. The face is undeniably ugly. It seems caught in a permanent snarl. Each of his bushy eyebrows forms an upside-down V, framing his emerald eyes. His pointed chin juts forward and the defect is heightened by the fact that it sports an untidy goatee. The mouse-brown hair surrounding it is tangled as if it hasn't been combed in centuries. Two small black horns protrude from either side of its unkempt depths. Every part of her wants to scream at this hideousness but she again catches sight of his eyes. They seem to reach out to her, saying, 'Do not fear me'. Her disgust for the creature is replaced by pity, his existence eternally caught between man and animal, not quite fitting into the world of either. As she gazes into his eyes she realises it is not menace reflected back at her, but love.

He breaks away, standing with his back to her. It is the guilt and remorse of his human part that overwhelms him now. With all his being he wants to keep her forever, simply for his pleasure, but he knows he must let her go and she will never return. Why should she? She is of her world, not his, and in her world he would be considered a beast. How could she love a beast?

The girl stares at him for a long time, and as she does so it appears to her that his form is no longer ugly but fine, noble and handsome. The fur on his legs and hooves is soft, velvety and warm. She tries to take him in her arms but he shies from her caresses. Slowly he allows her to touch him. She strokes the fur of his thigh and, as she does so, she feels his sex hardening once more. She takes it in both her hands. They look so small against the huge muscle. Still gripping it firmly, she lies back on the grass and guides him down on top of her. She opens her legs, allowing him to kneel in the V-shaped space between them. She bends her knees and pushes her pelvis off the ground, tilting her sex towards him. He is hesitant. She raises herself to her knees and places his sex at the entrance to her womb. Her smile encourages him. He penetrates her and this time her body is welcoming of his flesh. For her too the sensation is different. The movement is slow and he feels every inch of her flesh as it meets with his. She covers his face with kisses. She feels him stiffen inside her, forcing the tunnel of her sex to open wider still. There is a brief pinch of pain and then she is consumed with pleasure again. She gorges insatiably on his flesh and he on hers. The two forms melt into one being. Beauty and hideousness marry in an instant. He stares into her face and sees Syrinx staring back at him, no longer afraid or repulsed by his ugliness but smiling in adoration. The sunlight bathes them in a white light that seems to shine straight from the heavens. Afterwards he holds her tightly in his arms, his fur-lined legs entwined in her smooth ones. He stroked her hair gently as she slept, enjoying her closeness while it lasted.

When she awakes she is at the edge of the forest. Her mind is still tainted by the drunkenness of heavy sleep. The indigo hue of night is closing in around her. Her mother will be sick with worry by now. She remembers suddenly. She rises to her feet and glances in every direction. Her companion is nowhere to be seen. The woods have already been claimed by the dark and she can see no more than a few feet ahead of her. She does not know what else to do and so she starts for home.

She returned to the forest many times but she could never find her way back to the clearing. It is part of the inherent trickery of the woods that they look almost the same wherever you go. Often she stood perfectly still, listening carefully for any traces of a melody carried to her on the breeze. Occasionally she thought she heard a sliver of hollow notes, but when she listened more closely the only sound she heard was the song of a robin, chirping its tune from the branch of a nearby tree.

*Forbidden Fruit*

# Eden

*The serpent coiled tightly around the branch*
*And she understood what it said to her.*
*Tassssssste!*
*She lifted the fruit to her lips*
*Hesitating as she recalled the Great One's warnings.*
*Tasssssste!*
*As she bit into its flesh*
*Her innocence fell away from her*
*And her blindness.*
*She knew.*
*She knew of her body*
*Of her breasts*
*Of her womb*
*Of her cunt*
*And what it was for.*

*She could not keep her secret.*
*Her husband must also share this knowledge.*
*She offered him the fruit.*
*At first, he was angry with her*
*But then he ate.*
*He saw his body as a pillar of strength*
*And knew the purpose of the flesh between his legs.*
*The fruit fell from his hand as he took his wife.*
*They joined for the first time*
*Feeling the power of the union*
*Feeling pleasure like they had never yet been granted*
*Man into woman into man.*

*The Great One was incensed.*
*Furious at his children's disobedience*
*He cast them out*
*And as they ran from the garden*
*Hand in hand*
*They felt neither fear nor shame.*
*Banishment could not devastate them*
*For they now knew themselves*
*And how to attain true pleasure*
*With their bodies*
*A paradise that not even the Great One could prevent*
*They did not need his rationed happiness*
*He had denied them*
*But they would not deny themselves*
*They would create their own Eden*

# After the Ball

*Since I was a little girl I have loved fairytales. Even now I find it impossible to read them without slipping into their world and imagining myself as one of the characters. I love to read the stories in their original style, before they were sanitised by the Victorians. Before this time, fairytales were often sinister, gory and heavy with erotic metaphor. What else could the tale of Little Red Riding Hood be than the age-old story of a girl's first footsteps in the world of men, a world that her mother warns her about and wishes to protect her from? At this stage in my life, I can truly identify with her as I set forth on a similar journey (though I'm not sure how many wolves I'll meet along the way).*

*This fantasy is not based on Red Riding Hood but on another well-known fairytale (I will leave you to figure out which one). The question that held my interest was what happens after the happy ending. Is it possible for life to be too perfect? In this case the 'happily ever after' cannot hold as the princess finds herself feeling unworthy of the life she has acquired and seeking the cruel but familiar aspects of the life she has left behind. I believe that I would do the same.*

The princess had everything a young girl could wish for. She had her husband, a prince no less, who treated her with such tenderness and affection that the entire kingdom could be in no doubt of how much he loved her. She lived in a fine palace surrounded by every luxury imaginable. She had dozens of servants who knew instinctively what to bring her before she even had the chance to ask for it. As far as work was concerned, she never had to lift a finger. She was free to spend her days as she chose, lazing on her richly draped four-poster bed or taking leisurely walks through the castle grounds. Yet, amidst all this grandeur, the princess was not happy.

Often her mind would wander and she would dwell upon her old life in her stepmother's house. It was true that she had not been happy there either. Her stepmother had been cruel and she received nothing but spite and jealousy from her two stepsisters. They were unmistakably plain and resented her for her beauty. All three of them had treated her as a servant and tried to keep her hidden from the world outside the cottage. She had spent most of her time sitting amongst the cinders, wishing that a prince would sweep her onto the back of his horse and take her away to a new life. But it did not occur to her that she might actually get her wish.

She knew it was less than a year since she married the prince, but these days she could barely recall the peculiar circumstances under which she had said goodbye to the old cottage and its horrid inhabitants and become a royal princess. It all happened so suddenly that the memory of this reversal of lifestyle had become a hazy mirage that was never quite clear enough to make sense. She thought it must be her imagination playing tricks but she had a vague feeling it had involved pumpkins, mice and slippers.

How different her life was now! She had servants at her beck and call. Never again was she to kneel in the dirt whilst scrubbing the floor or to be scolded, beaten or abused with degrading nicknames.

She herself had changed. She had grown accustomed to the extravagances of life at the palace. She had become idle and greed had made her a touch plumper. At first she was grateful for everything she was given but now she expected it. After all, she was a princess!

It was during one of her walks, late in a long July afternoon, when she first saw him. He was on horseback, riding in her direction, his long hair cascading down his back like a waterfall of spun gold. A centaur! There was no man and no horse. There was only one being, the sculptured, olive muscles melting effortlessly into the silken hide. The most skilful artist could never have captured the grace of this rider and his ebony steed. But there was something else about him, something familiar like a long forgotten dream.

He pulled up the horse's reins not far from where she stood, and looked down at her from atop the animal. He was perhaps five or six years older than her, and wore such a sad expression that it made her forget who she was for a moment. But quickly she recovered and offered him a regal smile, expecting the traditional greeting of a lowering of eyes and reverent bowing of the head, fitting behaviour when one comes face to face with a princess.

Instead he held her gaze, silent and steadfast. Since she became a princess no one had dared to look at her in such a way. It was as though, with a simple look, the stranger had cut a substantial chunk out of the pedestal upon which she had been placed.

'What is your name?' she demanded. The rider made no reply but looked her up and down, taking in every detail of her robes and finery in what seemed to her to be a disapproving manner.

'Did you not hear me? I asked your name.' His silence filled her with unease but she could not deny that the person in front of her intrigued her. It was a rare man who would be so bold as to defy a princess.

Slowly his gaze shifted from her to the horse he rode. Pulling gently on the reins he turned it and began to ride away towards the old barn by the edge of the forest.

The princess seethed with rage and screamed after him. 'Stop! How dare you turn your back on me! I am the princess!'

She stamped her foot on the grass like a petulant child, sending a spatter of mud onto the hem of her expensive satin underskirt. For a split second she felt embarrassed; she had seen her stepsisters act this way so often. Had she really become as bad as them?

'I 'eard you scream, your majesty.' The princess spun around to see one of her serving maids scampering towards her. 'Is anything the matter?'

'Oh no, no, it is nothing really,' the princess answered, blushing deeply, and then a thought struck her. 'Tell me, that young man who rides away yonder, who is he?'

'Oh, that is just Manning, your highness,' the maid replied cheerily, proud that she knew something the princess did not. ''E lives out there in the old barn with a couple of 'orses and takes care of any poachers after the prince's stags. We don't see much of 'im. 'E keeps 'imself to 'imself, like.'

All through dinner that evening, the princess was distracted. The prince was concerned about her. He asked her if there was anything wrong, but she merely looked at the floor and shook her head. In truth she could not get Manning's face out of her mind. Why had he seemed so familiar? There was something about the way he looked at her with complete irreverence, even disgust. It made her feel like a nervous child. It was the same look that she had seen in the eyes of her stepmother and stepsisters, as though she were no better than the cinders amongst which she sat.

She retired early, complaining of a headache, and locked herself in her room. She buried herself in her bed and tried to let sleep take her away from Manning's vision, but every time she closed her eyelids she saw him staring back at her in that condescending manner. She knew she had to see him again, and she had to see him again that very night. She simply could not wait another day.

She bided her time, twisting in the sheets, until the rest of the house had gone to bed. Then when she had heard no sound for at least an hour, she slipped quietly from the warmth of her bed and pulled on her delicate Chinese-silk slippers. She remained in her pink satin nightdress with peacocks embroidered in gold, and wrapped herself in a black velvet cloak and hood.

Carefully, so as not to wake any of the servants, she crept out of her room and down the long hallway. It was filled with dozens of portraits of the prince's regal ancestors, and in the moonlight she could see their eyes frowning at her as though they were the eyes of her own conscience. She tried not to look at them, descending the spiral staircase and almost skidding on the polished marble floor downstairs. She knew the main door would be heavily guarded, and her only chance was the servants' exit. She tiptoed down another flight of stairs and through the large kitchen to the small wooden door. The latch lifted easily and she stepped out into the night.

She was free.

Hugging the cloak around her, she hurried through the palace grounds towards the old barn, and in the distance she could see the glow of a lantern from within. She hesitated once or twice, a million thoughts vying with each other in her head. What did she think she was doing? This was hardly appropriate behaviour for a princess, sneaking around in the middle of the night in her nightdress!

But something inside her drove her onwards. She reached the barn, and peering through the window she could see him, seated on a hay bale with his back to her, polishing one of the saddles. She realised it was not just his face that was familiar; it was everything about him – his arms, his posture, his movements as he worked.

There was no fire in the fireplace. The night was hot and there was no need of extra warmth. He worked in the light of a large lamp that had been placed on one of the old beams. In the far corner of the barn she could make out a stone corn mill. Nearby, she could see the two horses in their stalls. One was the muscular raven-coat she had seen him riding. The other was a simple workhorse, presumably used for pulling the heavy wooden lever around the mill to turn its grindstones.

Fighting the urge to turn back, the princess took a deep breath and stepped through the barn doors. The figure in front of her did not look round or even stop work, but his gruff voice cut the silence in half.

'What do you want?'

The words snapped at her like hounds. For a second her mouth dropped open in indignation and she readied herself for a tantrum. Then she remembered. She was not in the palace now. She had crossed the border from her world into his. She collected herself. She unbuttoned her cloak and hung it on one of the pegs by the door. She walked over and stood in front of him. Let him try to ignore her now!

His eyes did not lift from the saddle across his knee, and her heart sank.

'Well, aren't you going to bow and address me properly?' she asked.

Slowly he raised his head to look at her, his face full of scorn. '*I* bow to *you?* Well tell me, *princess*, what have you done lately that makes you worthy of my respect?'

She could not hold his gaze. She hung her head, feeling again like the little girl being scolded by her stepmother. It was as though she ceased to be a princess in his presence. It was a feeling of relief and it frightened her.

'Yes,' he said, 'you might well hang your head. All spoiled, selfish brats should hang their heads in shame.'

The words were like pinpricks, and she could no longer prevent her temper from exploding to the surface.

'What right do you have to speak to me like this?' she yelled. 'I am a princess! I am a thousand times more worthy than a filthy, stinking servant like you. I suppose it is too much to expect manners and refinement from a lowly beast! Look at you! Covered in soot, muck and manure! You should be grateful that I lower myself to look upon you!'

In a flash he had cast the saddle to the floor and leapt upon her. He grabbed her with both arms and shook her. She tried to run but he held her fast. He pressed his face inches from hers and she could see nothing but his pale grey eyes. She shut her own eyes tightly. His smell filled her nostrils. He smelt of leather and hay and wood. She felt his rough hands all over her, staining her body with their dirt, making her as filthy as he was. At first she shied from their touch, so used was she to keeping herself immaculately clean. Then, as the dirt was smeared onto her arms, legs and dress, she began to yield to them. She felt herself growing filthier and filthier but she did not fight against it any more. She had forgotten what it was like to feel dirty. His hands explored the hidden places up under her nightdress. Her legs began to part to allow them access.

Then suddenly guilt overwhelmed her. What was she doing? She grabbed his hands and prised them away with all her might, but he slapped her across the face and she was thrown by the suddenness of the painful impact to the dirty floor by the fireplace.

He turned his back on her so she could not read what was written in his face. She looked down at the dirt his hands had left on her thighs and again a feeling of familiarity swept over her. She wanted this. She wanted to be dirty – as dirty as sin.

Slowly she lowered herself onto her stomach in the grime and stretched out to rub against it. She began to writhe, first rigidly and then with more abandon. She rolled over and over in the soot until she was completely covered in it. She smeared it onto her face and in her hair. She wiped it all over her nightdress, turning the fragile material as black as the cinders themselves.

A rhyme she had heard when very young was plucked from her subconscious. Her mother, when she was still alive, read it to her from a large book of nursery rhymes. At first she struggled to collect all the words and arrange them in order, but finally she remembered it:

*Little Polly Flinders*
*Sat among the cinders*

*Warming her pretty little toes*
*Her mother came and caught her*
*And spanked her naughty daughter*
*For spoiling her nice new clothes*

Here she was, back among the cinders again, back in the same position that she had prayed to escape from for so many years. Far removed from being a regal princess, she was a nobody again; the lowliest of the low. She felt an unexpected sense of comfort and belonging. It was as though she had returned home to her rightful place after a long and wearisome journey through a foreign land.

There was only one thing missing now, and she glanced over at a large beam by the horses' stalls. Upon it hung a leather riding-crop. It was extremely worn and pieces of the pleated handle had begun to fray, but somehow she felt this was far more appropriate than a gleaming brand new one.

She looked at him with eyes pleading, even more desperate than when she had begged, long ago it seemed, for a gown in which to attend the prince's ball.

'Please,' she murmured, almost unable to force the words from her lips. 'Please will you beat me?' There. She had said it. And it felt good to grovel at the man's feet.

He turned and nodded solemnly. 'As you wish, your *royal highness.*' His sarcastic tone jolted her back to reality. All the duty, grace, refinement and snobbery that were expected of her as a princess flooded her conscience, but she pushed them away. Let her live as she had done before, if only for this moment.

She saw only his hand as he lifted the crop from the hook and walked towards her. She turned her face away, full of shame, excitement and joy at this homecoming. She knew her face betrayed all these emotions and she would not let him see. She faced the fireplace on her hands and knees and slowly rose to stand astride it as her stepmother had made her do, placing her hands securely on the mantel for support. Directly before her was an old mirror, and she gasped when she caught sight of her reflection. She could hardly recognise herself. She was filthy. Even more so than she had been at her stepmother's house. The black soot streaked her face, and her hair, normally so lustrously clean and prettily styled, was grimy and dishevelled. She seemed more animal than human.

'Quite a different picture you present now, princess.' Manning's reflection spoke to her from the glass. 'Yet this one is far more befitting your behaviour of late.' Taking two wooden clothes pegs, he lifted the material of her nightdress and secured it just above the small of her back, leaving the bare flesh of her buttocks unveiled. She wondered if he might tie her down, but he did not, and she realised it was more humiliating this way, to be made to stand there and take the punishment of her own free will.

She braced herself, desperate for the first stroke to fall and yet terrified of it. The reflection showed the crop being raised to shoulder height and hovering there for a dreadful moment, before its descent.

Then it swept down.

In the mirror she saw her own eyes widen as the spark shot into her exposed flesh. It fell again, swishing through the air and then landing with a crack across the padded globes of the royal bottom. Her knuckles, gripping the mantelpiece, had turned white with strain. In the stalls behind her the horses were startled at the noise and whinnied their anxiety. The crop landed again, two strikes in quick succession catching her on the backs of her legs. She bit her lip, trying desperately to stop the squeal from escaping them. What if one of the servants was to hear and to come and investigate? How could she explain this to the prince? Manning would surely be banished from the kingdom for something that was her own fault. So she swallowed her wails along with her pride.

Again and again the crop descended upon her. She was dizzy under the sting and the heat, but still she wanted more. It invigorated her. She could no longer stand still. He seemed to sense her agitation, and grabbing her by the wrist he threw her against the grindstone mill. She knew what she had to do. She placed her hands on the wooden lever and pushed against it with all her might. Slowly the mill began to turn. She started to push the lever round it in a circle. It was heavy, designed for the strength of a small horse. Her arms burned but the energy the crop had ignited in her body gave her strength.

Her punisher did not miss a beat. He continued to chastise her as she laboured, and his hand worked with its full power to drive her forward with the crop. The horses were restless, kicking nervously at their stable doors. In her own mind she became one of those horses, a humble beast of burden feeling the unforgiving implement biting into her rump as she toiled. She heard the sound of stone grinding stone and felt the joy of real work, a joy she had not felt since she left the old house. She was soaked wet with sweat. Every muscle in her body ached deliciously, until finally exhaustion overwhelmed her.

She staggered over to the fireplace and collapsed in a heap among the cinders. Manning hung the crop back in its place and then came to stand over her.

'Who are you?' she whispered, daring to glance for a moment at his face. 'I have seen you before. I know you.'

'Yes, Cinders, you do.' The old familiar nickname slapped her in the face. 'And I know you. I know who you are and, more importantly, I know who you *were!* I looked after your father's stables when you were a little girl. I was only a young lad myself but I thought you were the most beautiful girl I had ever seen. I saw how the house changed when your mother died and your father remarried. Your stepmother sent me away but I kept returning to the house, watching you grow up. I saw the way they treated you. I heard their constant scolding. I watched through the window as you were beaten and even shed tears in sympathy with your own. Despite all of these ills thrust upon you, your heart remained innocent, pure and selfless. I admired that.'

He paused, seeming to choke on the words, and when he spoke again his voice was greatly altered. All of the gentleness had drained from it, leaving it bitter.

'Now look at you. Leading the wonderful new life you always dreamed about, showered with gifts and luxuries, everything done for you. Servants to wipe your royal arse! You never realised how much these riches would change you, did you, Cinders? They have transformed you from a sweet and innocent girl into a spoiled brat. You are worse than your stepsisters were and you know it! Everybody scrapes and bows and tells you that you are better than you really are and you have started to believe it. That is why you came here tonight. That is why you crave humiliation such as this. That is why you begged me to punish you. It is the first beating you have ever received that you truly deserve!'

Her face was stained with tears. The truth wounded her far worse than the crop had done. He was right, though she had not realised it until now. She curled into a ball, hid her face in her arms and let the tears flow. He stood calmly beside her as she cried, and when she lifted her head again she knew what she wanted.

She rose to her feet, facing him with her arms by her side. He looked directly into her eyes and seemed to know what they asked of him. His hands reached out and gripped the dirt-encrusted material of her nightdress, his fists whitened as he ripped it away to reveal her pale flesh beneath, and he cast the garment onto the hay in the corner of the barn.

For her it was as though she were a butterfly emerging from a too long encasement in the safety of her cocoon. She no longer wanted its sanctuary; she wanted the world outside with all its dangers.

She stood for a moment, allowing him to take in her nakedness. She turned slowly, giving him a complete view of her body. His eyes traced every detail of her breasts, buttocks and sex, and his hand came to rest on the top of her head. He clenched his fist, gripping a handful of her sodden hair, and slowly he pushed her down to kneel at his feet.

Without being told to she reached up and unbuttoned Manning's breeches, and slid her hand inside to feel his penis. It was already hard and she tugged it out to gaze upon it. He did not let go of her hair but guided her face to it, and obediently she parted her lips and took it between them. She tasted the salty juices as they began to flow. Her hair fell about her face as her head rocked back and forth. Her tongue worked rigorously over every inch of her prize, feeling it swell under her wet caresses. She took his testicles into her mouth, sucking them gently as she frigged his cock with dedicated hands. She licked his manhood from its base to its tip, smothering it in her saliva, allowing her wetness to combine with his. Her mouth readied him and she prepared herself to offer him her other place. She was no longer princess but whore, and felt more honour and dignity in that role.

He let go of her hair, pushing her forehead so that she lay back on the dusty floor. She spread her legs wide and her cunt opened like the petals of a flower to welcome him. He straddled her on his knees and eased his sex into hers. Her hands grasped for him, pulling him down on top of her. No more denial. They made love as though they were animals.

No, this was not making love.

This was fucking.

It was nature taking its course, an instinct that had existed since man had taken his first steps out of the primordial slime in the dawn of time. Sex with the prince had always been so sterile, so clinical, but now she rolled with her lover over and over across the barn floor. Mud and hay stuck to their sweat-ridden skin. Her body cried out to him, telling him how much she wanted him. Her pleasure, dormant for so long, rose to a height she had never felt before. His cock conquered her and she welcomed the defeat.

He pulled out of her and sat upon her breasts while her own hands took over, hungrily probing her vagina. He made her work for her satisfaction, slapping his rigid sex across her face. His creamy liquid sprayed all over her, drenching her, washing away the dirt and soot from her nose, cheeks and mouth. She lapped at it, swallowing as much as she could. Her own juices saturated her fingers.

She shrieked her orgasm from her gut, no longer caring who heard, and then curled up in the hay, pressing her fingers over her pulsating sex.

Manning raised one foot and let it rest gently on her spine, and there, beneath his worn and muddy boot, she felt protected and in her rightful place.

The horse galloped, its hooves echoing through the night. The moon lit their path. She clung tightly to Manning. Her tender bottom bounced against the saddle so that she could feel every mark the crop had branded onto it. She felt warm and loved. She knew the prince would search for her as he had done before but she would make certain that he did not find her. This time she had left him her filthy nightdress rather than a pristine slipper of glass. She felt sorry for him. It was not his fault that she could not stay. He had given her everything she wanted but could not give her what she needed.

She did not know where they were going, and she did not care as long as it was away. Away from everything! Away from stepmothers and poverty and filth. Away from palaces and royalty and attention. She had experienced life at both extremes of the spectrum and could find contentment at neither end.

She pressed her lips against Manning's back and rode onwards to a life somewhere in between.

# The Task

*I find the idea of initiation and ritual very heavily linked with eroticism. After all, sex itself is one of the oldest rituals of all. Likewise, the act of giving or receiving punishment is also a kind of ceremony involving distinct preparatory steps: the removal of clothing, the securing of the receiver in position, the anticipation and finally the first strike of the hand, cane, strap, etc.*

*I often fantasise about being the victim of such a ritual as I describe in the story. This fantasy explores the idea not of the virgin sacrifice but the sacrifice of virginity. Ro's journey is equivalent to that of any other girl as she is initiated into the customs of adult eroticism.*

She knew she would be chosen. Everyone knew. Each year, one month before the winter solstice, the villagers selected the most beautiful of all their maidens to complete the Task. The harvest must come and the gods must be appeased. The beauty of Ro's mother, in her day, was spoken of throughout the land, and all her five daughters had inherited that beauty.

Every one of Ro's older sisters had been chosen for the Task as she came of age, just as their mother had completed it a generation before. Now Ro, the last of the succession, would have her turn.

A tremendous excitement swept the whole village during the days leading up to the Election. It was widely agreed that Ro's beauty surpassed that of any of her fine sisters.

It would surely be a year of plenty if only she performed her duty well.

In the early days the girls had been chosen through a kind of lottery. As it became obvious that the gods valued beauty and innocence before all other attributes, the lottery was replaced by a simple system of election. Each adult member of the village would write the name of their choice on a slip of parchment and place it into the woven sack that hung outside the Elder's hut. The votes were then counted and, at the weekly gathering, the Elder would announce the name of the chosen girl. Ro's mother was the first to be elected in such a way, and that year the harvest was one of the richest the village had ever seen, and so the system remained in place for the years to follow.

Perhaps the method was a little less fair than the lottery, but at least it ensured that only the most beautiful were given the Task. The gods would be satisfied and a generous harvest would be granted.

Although she was not surprised when her name was read out, Ro felt as though she had swallowed a heavy stone. She did not protest; she knew the moment had been inevitable, written into her destiny since the day she was squeezed from her handsome mother's womb. She had dreaded it and yet was filled with a curious excitement, even pride. It meant she was finally a woman and time had come for her to face her future and her fate. Few of the village's maidens were given the honour of such an important role, such a vital contribution to the welfare of her people, and she prayed she would be worthy of the Task. Could she really perform it to the gods' satisfaction?

During the past four years she had watched each of her sisters take the Task in their turn. She saw their eyes moisten and heard their cries ascending into the night sky.

She had also noticed the blissful smile that grew across their lips when all was completed, and she wondered why. Could it be the joy of having been of service to the village? Or was it something else, something mysterious, integral to the Task itself?

She had questioned each of her sisters incessantly during the weeks that followed, but they simply smiled and told her she would know when her time came. She missed her sisters dearly. She wished they were there to reassure her, but they had all found husbands and moved away with them to other villages.

Her mother comforted her, stroking her forehead gently until she fell asleep each night, but she would not give away anything about what it felt like to complete the Task.

'You must discover for yourself, little one,' she would whisper.

Ro had but twenty-eight risings of the sun to make herself ready for the Task, and for the whole of that time she was to be treated as though she were a queen. She would be fed nothing but the freshest crops and the most succulent portions of the hunters' kill. She would have the finest materials to sleep on at night. Two maidens of the same age were assigned the duty of preparing her body. Every evening they bathed her in fresh milk and nectar, and how luxurious this felt compared with her usual ice-cold baths in the river!

Afterwards they would dab her dry and lay her out on her back on the rug by the fire. They would pour over her a jug of richly scented oils and stroke her from fingertip to toe. They would smooth the oil over her breasts, over her flat stomach and through her downy tuft of dark hair to her toned thighs. Then they would playfully flip her over onto her stomach, giggling as they traced their slender fingers down her spine and over the magnificent curves of her buttocks, thankful that their job required them to concentrate on this area.

They knelt beside her, one on each side, and ran their palms up her shapely legs and over the well-formed arcs. Occasionally they would allow their fingers to dip between the excellent orbs. They would whisper teasingly in her ear, tell her how much they longed to watch her complete the Task and how devotedly they would administer to her afterwards. Ro would simply giggle and turn red. She liked their secret whispers and the sensation that their inquisitive hands produced in her.

The time went by with great speed and finally the evening of the ceremony arrived. Her nervous excitement had become more intense as the day went on. All the questions that had buzzed in her head ever since she was tiny and her mother had told her of the Task were to be answered this night. How slowly the sun god had ridden through the sky today!

By the time her two handmaidens arrived to prepare her she could barely speak. They bathed and oiled her. They helped her into the ceremonial dress, which had been made just for her. It was the most beautiful she had ever seen, let alone worn. The pure white fabric was so soft and gauzy that she could not stop running her fingers over it. She gazed at her reflection and saw how lovingly it clung to her, displaying every curve and leaving no doubt that she was, at last, a woman. Through the material she could easily see the shape of her nipples and the small triangle of hair below her navel.

The girls scolded her for dawdling and sat her down. They combed and braided her long brunette tresses, entwining them with fresh flowers. They painted her face, reddening the lips and applying black around the eyes and lashes to make them seem as dark and mysterious as the night itself.

Last of all they strapped the heavy collar of iron around her slender neck, as was the custom, threading thick rope through the loop at the front. But they need not have bothered, for she would not run.

When they heard the drums summoning Ro, they led her through the village streets towards the hill. The villagers stared at her as she passed, then came flocking out of their huts to follow the solemn procession. She stepped proudly, head high and elegant, eyes locked straight ahead. The drums pounded out their steady, purposeful rhythm. She could see the familiar scene before her, the Priest waiting patiently before the tall wooden frame, dressed in the traditional scarlet cloak and white mask of a holy-man. Nearby the grey stone of the altar was set alive with the firelight of a hundred candles scattered around its perimeter.

She came to a standstill on the hilltop in front of the holy-man. She knelt on one knee, head bowed in reverence. The rest of the village gathered around them, the heads of each family brandishing a flaming torch. As she glanced upward she could see the flames reflected through the eyeholes of the Priests mask as if his very eyes were made of that same fire.

The two handmaidens untied the rope and went to take their place with their families. The Priest paused for a long while scrutinising her, and then gradually lifted his arms to the heavens.

'Almighty masters, another year has passed and we again bring you an offering. In humble thanks we present you with the most precious jewel we have to give. We pray that your eyes are upon her as she endures the Task you have decreed in written lore since the dawn of time. We pray that you grant us prosperity worthy of her sacrifice!'

His gaze fell upon her once again, and she rose to follow him as he walked over to the frame and stood, still and silent, before it. She had seen it many times before, but never from so close an angle. Every year it was assembled in the same way. Three large stakes, as tall as a hut, were bound together at one end to form a pyramid. Their ends were then burrowed into the ground to keep the frame sturdy. It seemed so much bigger from so close – so much more menacing.

The Priest circled round behind her and seized the material of her dress on either shoulder, then with one swift, solid movement he ripped the dress in two. The vision of her nakedness flew into every eye. A whisper of awe passed through the crowd, for the loveliness of her figure did indeed match that of her face.

She waited passively while the village stared at her, feeling their eyes feasting on every part of her. The cold bit into her skin but she knew this would not last long.

The Priest wasted no time. Grabbing her wrists he bound them securely. The harsh rope gripped cruelly against the tender, oil-soaked flesh. Hooking the other end of the rope over the top of the frame, he hoisted her hands high above her head until she could only touch the ground on tiptoe and secured them in place.

From within his robes the Priest produced a long leather strap. He held it with both hands, lifting it heavenwards. All the young men of the village came forward to form a circle around the frame. All eyes were fixed upon the exposed, delicate flesh, washed as white as the milk it had bathed in. The Priest again addressed the gods.

'Masters, guide our hands with your strength. Help us purify her body in preparation for the Task.'

The Priest strode over and stood just behind Ro. She could not see him but could feel the heat of his breath on her bare skin. She quivered, never feeling so helpless, a mere pawn in the hands of fate.

'Suffer well, my child,' he whispered. 'The gods are watching.' Then with a sound that could have woken the gods themselves, the Priest brought the strap down across the waiting girl's magnificent buttocks. Her luscious mouth fell open with the shock of the assault, and one-by-one each man in the circle stepped forward to take the strap and deliver a blow, each branding her with his own mark on the place of his choosing. Some of them concentrated, as the holy-man had done, on the plump target that her buttocks provided, some scalded her lithe back where her flesh was less protecting. Some chose to blight her smooth white breasts, making sure that each one flushed as pink as her rear. Her whole body, from her breasts to her calves, burned like the torch flames. Each new strike intensified the pain. Each blow cleansed her, made her more pure in the eyes of the gods. Tears streamed down her cheeks. She could no longer feel her wrists, chaffed raw by the rough ropes. Her howls soared upwards into the ebony sky. The Priest screamed his encouragement.

'Sing, little bird. Sing to the gods!'

The village women danced excitedly. They were certain the gods would hear and would be impressed.

When every member of the circle had taken his turn, the Priest again took up the leather and delivered a tremendous final cut across her flesh. Then casting the strap aside he untied the rope and freed her numb hands, and she felt as though she would swoon as the blood rushed back into them.

He lifted her and carried her over to the stone altar to complete the Task. He lay her on her back and spread her legs wide, revealing her virgin maidenhood. Her back arched as she pressed her throbbing buttocks into the soothing coolness of the stone. Lifting the heavy iron cuffs at each corner of the stone, he fastened them first to her ankles and then to her wrists so that her body formed a cross, stretched akimbo over the altar.

Her breathing quickened. She was totally vulnerable, her body a vessel at the mercy of man and god alike. This was the moment she had been most wary of, but now it had arrived she was unafraid. The beating had stirred her blood and her loins. She welcomed the Task.

Slowly the crowd began to chant the age-old words.

*'Plant the seed. Grow the fruit. Plant the seed. Grow the fruit.'*

Climbing onto the altar to kneel between her knees, the Priest parted his robe. Through her tear-blurred eyes she saw his manhood as hard as the stone itself. What an honour to be stabbed with such a weapon! She wanted to feel it in the place where none had yet ventured. She could feel the juices stir within her body, readying it.

He entered her, and she let out such a cry as he pierced through the flesh, wedging it open, that several of the onlookers stopped their chanting to gasp in awe. She felt as though she were being torn in two like her dress. Deep pain, the like of which she had never felt, but mixed with such sweetness! The iron held her in place. The two bodies began to thrust as though engaged in some primitive dance to the rhythm of the chant. Plant the seed. Grow the fruit. Plant the seed. Grow the fruit. She lifted her pelvis, opening wide to take him. He thrust deeper, forcing her wider still. She could make out his eyes behind the mask. They pierced her in the same way. The opening of her womb began to relax. It grew hungrier for him with every movement. She thrashed wildly, lost in the ancient, ancient act, gripping his hardness and pulling it further in.

The stone beneath her grazed her skin but she did not notice. She felt nothing but the burning deep within her, and at last the Priest shot forth his seed into her belly. She felt the hot liquid gush into her, filling her completely, and a second later her own juices leaked from her, mixing with his.

She screamed out her pleasure to the gods. The Task was complete.

Afterwards Ro's handmaidens helped her down from the altar. They would stay with her, nursing her wounds with special herbs for as long as they took to heal. She glanced down at the stone stained with her own blood, the mark of the chaste and the chastened. She realised she was wearing that same smile that she had seen on her sisters' faces. The seed had indeed been planted, and she knew the harvest would be as fruitful as her womb had become.

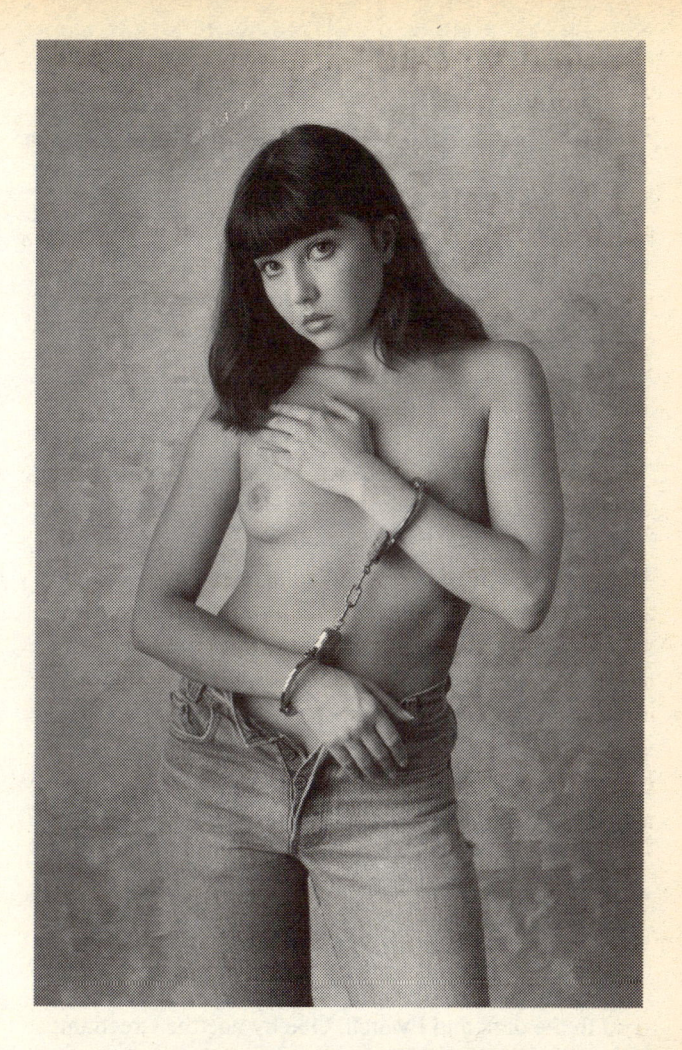

*Captured Innocence*

# The Watcher

*This fantasy reflects the way I see myself at this stage of my life. I am constantly watching the promiscuous goings on of the world from a safe distance, enjoying lovely daydreams about participating in them but never actually doing so. I enjoy keeping the fantasy alive for as long as possible, unspoilt by reality. I also love the idea of being the object of voyeuristic individuals. It is probably the actress in me coming out but the idea of an audience excites me. Lots of women, I am told, have fantasies about becoming a stripper and it does not surprise me at all. When I was younger I was watching television and caught a glimpse of a pole-dancer, clad in nothing but a tiny g-string, gyrating her arse for the erotic entertainment of drooling male punters. In the split second before my parents hastily flicked over the channel, I had wished I were she.*

*I want to be ogled, desired, lusted after while I show off my wares. I am not at all bothered by what my audience looks like. In actual fact, I find the idea of a dirty old man far more of a turn on than that of a trendy guy my own age. A dirty old man would let me be dirty myself and wouldn't be shocked if I turned out to be dirtier than he was.*

I sit in the dark and I watch. One by one the streetlamps flicker on to herald the coming night. The amber glow filters through the open shutters creating a griddle of light on my bedroom wall. I shift into a kneeling position in the middle of my bed so I can see out of the window. Beside me are my binoculars, a present for my fifteenth birthday and, as it turns out, one of the most useful I have ever been given, though not quite for the purpose they were intended.

From here I can see the entire view laid out in front of me like a theatrical stage. I have the perfect seat from which to enjoy the show. There it is – the block of flats across the street from my apartment, a metropolis of little windows, each one a portal providing a glimpse into the lives of its occupants, each with its own enigmatic story waiting to be discovered, a world of gossip and intrigue and just the thing to entertain a keen and curious girl.

The evening is closing in fast. Soon the show will begin.

I live alone in my eighth-floor apartment on the Rue Blanche. Well, I like to tell people it's mine – it sounds so grown-up – but I confess that it is really papa who pays my rent, determined as he was that I should not live in any shabby, drug-ridden student accommodation. I am sure he would not approve if he realised the apartment I have selected is situated in the Place de Clichy, at the centre of Paris's red light district!

I feel no guilt. Apart from the money for my rent and a reasonable weekly allowance, he needs part with no more. I do not pay any fees for my education, though it is the best the city has to offer. My scholarship at the college was assured. I didn't even send them my best work, merely a few sketches and a couple of oils on canvas. The phone call came practically the next day and I was packed off to Paris to begin the course within a month.

I must say that the course itself is not what I had hoped it would be. The current module is life art. Ha! I use the title with much sarcasm. I was excited, at first, at the prospect of drawing naked men, staring at every detail, my pencil leaving no part unnoticed, but the models are always so lifeless, as physically limp as they are mentally. They are sun-bedded, would-be Adonises with rock hard layers of rippling muscles who stand in stagnant, sterile poses, completely dead between the legs. I draw them as I am supposed to but it is as though they were bowls of fruit. My life lessons only truly begin when I step out of the college door.

My apartment is compact, but more than adequate for one girl. When I lean out from the window I can see the bright, neon-coated sails of the Moulin Rouge which turn seductively every night as if they were fingers beckoning in the lonely and the curious.

I have never been to the show there. What would be the point when I have such a spectacle performed for me through the un-curtained windows opposite? It is my very own dolls house, one in which the dolls are alive and move themselves. No stage full of long-legged women jiggling desperately with painted-on smiles could compete with the private lives of my dolls. They dance for free, every night, for my entertainment. And they do so much more than just dance! I am Alice, already down the rabbit hole and looking with aching curiosity through the tiny doorway at the mysterious and elusive gardens of Wonderland.

A burst of laughter is carried up from the street below, and glancing down I see a young couple tumbling out of the Museum of Sex. They are squeezing each other tightly and giggling like two schoolchildren. As they continue their journey his palm coils like a serpent around her buxom waist and comes to land on the curve of her bum. Its shape fills his hand perfectly.

I sigh. The museum's dark interior remains as much a

mystery to me as sex itself, for nothing save my own inquisitive fingers has probed my virginity. I walk right past its dildo-filled windows on my way home from college each afternoon. One time I paused to look at them. They reminded me of candy, all colours and shapes. Some were obviously made to resemble that part of the male anatomy that they were designed to compensate for. Others had funny, knobbly tops that looked a bit like sea anemones. I didn't have a clue what you were supposed to do with those. There was even one that was shaped and coloured like a banana! I wondered if it tasted like one too.

The thought crossed my mind to march right in there and purchase one of them. Why not? My allowance was ample and it would only take a moment to nip in through the door. But I was working up the courage to do so when a middle-aged couple appeared out of the shop next-door and eyed me up and down in disapproval. My cheeks flushed scarlet. The grey-haired woman, a prototypical cranky aunt, creased her brow and scolded me in her thick French tongue.

'Go home, child!'

A hint of a grin on her husband's lips vanished only when his portly spouse turned in his direction, and I could not help smirking myself as I scurried, ruefully, into my apartment block.

My mind snaps out of my reminiscence with the sharp trap-trapping of stiletto heels upon the pavement. My Lady approaches, pounding the cement with the same vigour that she uses to pound the eager backsides of her multitude of adoring clients. For she is a dominatrix. I am certain that is the right word. No common prostitute is she, though she surely gives as much pleasure as the most experienced of whores. She rounds the corner, leading her client by the arm. Her stark, peroxide hair is pulled back in a neat ponytail and her smart PVC bolero is just a touch more modest than her red latex miniskirt.

Her companion wears sunglasses like they all do. I know that, beneath them, his eyes are blindfolded. She is clever and will remove it only when they are safely inside the apartment, making certain he does not discover the address. Besides, it is all part of the fun, the mystery.

Who is it this time? I strain my eyes through the lenses to see. A regular? No, someone new. He has no idea what lies in store for him. But I do. Her apartment is opposite and one story down. I see everything.

Maybe it is the artist in me, but I have been fascinated, even obsessed with her and what she does since the moment I first turned my binoculars towards her flat and saw her riding her client like a horse, whipping his buttocks as he cleaned her flat. There are so many questions I long to ask her. Does she enjoy her work? Does she do it purely for money? After all, they pay her a small fortune and bring her expensive gifts as well. I am sure that, for her, the money is a bonus. I bet she adores being worshipped and taking out her frustrations on her clients. I do not know why I find the concept so appealing but I rather fancy I would like to try it myself. I do not mean being a dominatrix. It is strange but I never imagine myself in her role. I am always the grovelling slave beneath her feet, feeling her smooth buttocks cushioned into my back as I dust and scrub for her. I have never yet seen her dominate a woman. Perhaps I would be her first. What would it be like to serve her, to feel her boot on my head and her whip on my flesh? She would still treat me with contempt but would be secretly pleased at the novelty of having soft curves under her control instead of the rough, square bodies she is accustomed to.

I love to paint her. She is my favourite subject though she does not know it. I capture her when she is at her most terrible, her face full of fury as she screams at her incompetent slaves. I sometimes draw them too, cowering, blubbering for mercy as their back and buttocks redden under her cruel whip. Once I even submitted one of my pictures of her to my tutor for assessment, only to be told the subject matter was inappropriate for a girl my age. I didn't care. I was just happy to have been able to share her beauty with someone else. The tutor never returned the picture.

On occasion I tease myself, mockingly, with the notion of actually going over there to knock at her door, perhaps take her one of my paintings. But no, some fantasies are as delicate as fine crystal and must live as they are or be shattered beyond repair. And so I stay safely enclosed in my apartment. I am content to imagine myself in the shoes of every new client who comes grovelling to her doorway and part with his cash for a taste of her whip, a taste of escapism. I play a new role every time but it is always the same one, that of an insect before a Queen.

A light flickers on in the room below hers. It belongs to a young couple in their early thirties; Italian, I believe. They moved in just after I did, about three months ago and I have already watched them in their intimacies countless times. Sometimes they leave the windows open and I can hear his baritone grunts quite clearly.

I am certain they are newlyweds. They divide their time equally between passionate arguing and passionate fucking. Tonight there is no doubt which one it will be. They rip each other's clothes off within seconds of coming through the door. His strong, hairy arms lift her and drop her onto the bed. What position will they adopt? Doggy-style, eh? That seems to be their favourite. I watch them closely. I like the shape her body makes as she waits for him to enter her, her large bosom swinging freely beneath her. I look down at the small bumps on my chest. How I wish I had breasts like hers! They make her look so womanly, so full of sex.

He pauses a moment to drink in the enticing image she presents him with. Please open the window. Open it. Please! I want to hear this one. Yes! Here he comes. He opens it wide and then turns back to his eager prize. He is erect even before his trousers are off. He kicks them away and kneels behind her. His hand guides his cock into place and her eyes widen as their bodies join and begin to grind. The wind carries their moans from the window and into my inquisitive ears. The old woman in the room below them yells some obscenity and slams her window shut. I can understand her annoyance. They can go on for an hour sometimes. I burst with jealousy. I have so much yet to experience.

But then again, I am not as innocent as I seem. I have secrets of my own.

The businesswoman is home. Her apartment is always a little difficult to see. Although it is level with mine, it is on the end of the building and she always keeps the lamps down low. In some ways I find her even more intriguing than my dominatrix. She always arrives home in such refined attire – thin, gold-rimmed spectacles, a neatly pressed blouse, smart slacks and pristine business jacket. I imagine her to be the head of a massive corporation somewhere in the financial district. I laugh to think of her holding board meetings at the end of a long, polished table, yelling at her board of executives if the profits are down this month compared with last. If only they knew what I know! If only her work colleagues could see what a different person she becomes behind her own locked door!

Her apartment is a Mecca for beautiful ladies, different ones all the time. I am desperate to know where she meets them all. Elegant parties? Or seedy lesbian nightclubs in the back alleys, just off the Rue de Douai? No, I am certain it is neither of these. I like to think that she hires them from a regular brothel just as a man would, trying out a new flavour every time. Perhaps she fears commitment and it is easier this way, to simply enjoy sexual pleasure without a relationship interfering with her career. What a lovely surprise for the ladies themselves to feel the tender caresses of an attractive woman instead of the clumsy groping hands they must be used to!

Her ladies are of all nationalities and all sizes and shapes – tall blondes, slim brunettes, shapely redheads. They all knock on her door and greet her with a kiss and a smile when she opens it. They all wear long coats and remove them to reveal skin-tight dresses or steamy-looking lingerie. She threads her arms around their waist and presses her mouth to theirs, a spider ensnaring its prey.

They kiss with the tongue, as is the French custom for lovers. Her hands slide up and down their velvet bodies. Their hands, in turn, reach out to unbutton her jacket and blouse, loosening her bra to free her breasts. They massage the excited flesh.

Sometimes two or three ladies arrive on her doorstep. I am always disappointed in these cases, for she leads them into her chamber, closing the door behind her. What mysteries she and her lovers get up to behind that door I can only imagine. But occasionally, when she entertains only one guest, she remains in the kitchen where I can see her. She bends them back over the kitchen table and peels off each item of clothing with relish as though peeling an exotic fruit. She takes off her spectacles and pulls the combs from her auburn hair, letting it cascade over their stomach. She sways her head up and down, teasing them, trickling the silky hair over their faces and breasts, down the length of their body to their feet. There she employs her eager tongue, lovingly sucking each of their toes. She moves up past their ankles to their calves. Then to their inner thighs where she remains for a little while, teasing them. They spread their legs wider, willing her tongue higher still. They seem to know what is in store. Perhaps the other girls have briefed them on her tastes, jealously wishing she would book them again.

At last she hits the target. She buries her face in their pussies and they let her go to work. She knows exactly how to please them. Her hands pleasure herself at the same time. Sometimes they close their thighs, gripping her head like a vice to pull her into them. Sometimes they place their hands on her head, clasping her hair in a clenched fist as they offer her their juices. She laps them up like a cat.

One girl, who must have been a gymnast or something, lifted her legs up and back over her shoulders whilst being licked. She looked stunning, her short, raven bob highlighting the creaminess of her skin. I have had many lovely fantasies about her, imagining all the kinds of positions she could get into to have sex with her clients. I was certain the businesswoman would ask her back again, but like all the rest, she was invited to the apartment once and only once.

I look up towards the butcher's window. I know he's a butcher because I saw him once in his little one-man shop, just behind the Sacre Coeur. Peering through the glass I could see his large hands and brow covered in sweat as he carved heartily into a succulent ham. It made me laugh to think that this savage brute was the same man who had prepared and displayed, with the utmost delicacy, the splendid window display of Falette, vol-a-vents and other delicious comestibles. Primitive hunter and refined artist in one!

It was through the window of the butcher's apartment, a month previously to the day, that I made an intriguing discovery. It seems I am not alone in my voyeuristic pleasures. A watcher is watching the watcher, and at first glance I almost dropped my binoculars as they suddenly met with the fixated lens of the butcher's telescope. And I guess he was just as startled, because when I looked again his shutters had been drawn and I did not see him again that night.

The following evening he ventured to his telescope again, and I imagined that he craved his nightly entertainment as much as I did. I again turned my binoculars towards his window, but this time he did not vanish but remained there staring as though directly into my eyes, scrutinising me. I took a deep breath. I had no doubt what I was going to do.

With slow deliberation I pulled up my blind completely so there was nothing to hinder his view but a thin sheet of naked glass. I turned on my lamp. It was not bright but provided sufficient illumination for my purpose. I checked to make certain he had noticed. He had, and this was the beginning of what was to become our daily ritual.

His window is two stories higher than mine so I knew he could see all of my bed and at least half of my room. Carefully I placed my binoculars on my bedside cabinet and sat upright on the bed. With my back to my solitary audience I peeled my tight T-shirt up and over my head. I never bother with a bra. I reached up and unwound my hair from its tightly bound braids, letting its dark, chestnut tresses cascade about my shoulders and over my pert, teardrop breasts. I spun to face him once more, allowing a flash of pink and of delicate, erect nipple before the hair settled in place again.

I stole a glance through my binoculars. As I expected, his shutters had been closed to narrow slits with his telescope's lens shoved intrusively through. I could make out his shape through the shutter's gaps. He was not attractive in the general sense. He was balding, middle-aged and more than slightly overweight. But he could give me what those impotent models at the college could not. He was alive. His flesh was real flesh, responsive and erect. I watched as his hand gripped himself and began to pump with a slow, regular motion, the reaction produced by the sight of me, a girl undressing!

I was so full of pride that I started to giggle. It was rude and wonderful. My treasured virginity now penetrated, simply and effectively, by a pair of eyes.

I lay back again, and arching my limber spine I undid the buttons of my faded jeans and slid the clinging material down my thighs, over my ankles to join my T-shirt on the floor. I was left with nought but my crisp, sky-blue panties with the tiny roses on them. For a moment I wished I had something more provocative, black lacy ones perhaps, but I was sure he wouldn't mind.

Rolling onto my stomach I thrust my bottom into the air like a cat, giving my ogling onlooker an excellent view of the taut, rounded curves. I reached back and pulled the material into the deep cleft between my buttocks, a self-made G-string just like the ones they wore at the Moulin Rouge. So this is what it felt like to be one of the dancers, swirling my ass around, allowing it to squirm teasingly before ravenous eyes. I began to writhe; circling my hips and thrashing my thick mop of dark hair this way and that. I began to perform – to really perform. I was swept up in my performance, smiling at the ironic turnaround. Voyeur had now become exhibitionist. I had never before felt arousal like this. Despite the many times I'd watched others, I had never known the excitement of being watched myself.

Twisting onto my back and spreading my legs wide, I slid my hand into the front of my panties. He would be able to see it disappearing and its movement against the tight cotton, but still no glimpse of the place where it went. I hooked my thumbs into the elastic and began to lower it, but I stopped just below the edge of my pubic hair. No, I thought, not yet. One day soon, but not today. Don't give him everything at once. Leave him hungry for more.

I thrilled at the tease. I could feel my button of tender flesh swelling and stiffening. I sucked my fingers, covering them with moist, slippery saliva. Eagerly my hand darted down into my knickers again, tracing the flesh they hid. I closed my eyes and imagined it was his tongue I could feel gliding here and there with all the expertise of an older man. I moved my pelvis up and down in the time old rhythm of sexual intercourse I had seen the Italian couple adopt so often. My hair slid back, exposing my breasts completely but I no longer cared. My gyrations became more vigorous. I wondered what it would be like to have his penis inside me. Its stiff rod pushing in, way back where my fingers couldn't reach.

To smell his sweat and feel the weight of his body over me as we fucked. To be his whore, his dirty girl, ripe and ready for the taking. My orgasm rose and spilled into my panties soaking the material with hot, sweet-scented liquid. My whole body bucked like a rodeo horse and my fingers came to rest.

When I glanced again at his window the butcher was gone and the shutters closed for the night, and I guessed that, warm and fulfilled, he had gone to take a bath.

Thus we indulge ourselves in this strange erotic ceremony every evening. We are locked in our cyclic game. Both know the rules. We never meet or even speak with each other. As with my dominatrix, the practicalities of a real encounter would spoil everything. Besides, there is a deep sensuality in denial itself, in waiting for pleasure. Sometimes I perform for him. Sometimes I reverse the show and become the audience again. I sit stubbornly with my binoculars and do not move until he turns on his light and pulls his hard shaft just for me.

Recently he has been leaving little packages in my letterbox. I never run into him. Maybe he drops them off in his lunch hour, but they are always there when I return home from college. There is never any note accompanying them. I guess he leaves me to imagine whatever romantic words from him that I wish. They are always small gifts, offerings perhaps, like the clients of my dominatrix bring for her – stockings of fine silk, lacy suspender belts, satin basques, see-through negligees – all of which I joyfully model for him on the evening of their receipt.

Sometimes I give him a private striptease. I unhook the stocking, sliding it down my thigh like I've seen the movie stars do, bending my knee as the silk glides over it, down over my calf and then my pointed toes. I love all the clothes he buys for me. I look in the mirror and I'm reminded of one of my businesswoman's ladies of the night. The clothes enhance my femininity, showing off my lithe body. Whenever I put on such garments, the feel of them somehow influences my behaviour. It is like being under a spell. I feel like a bad girl and want to act like I feel. My shyness melts away. My shows for him grow raunchier. No longer do my panties stay on, prudishly shielding my secret parts. I slip them down over my round bottom, sticking it out provocatively as I do so. Everything is then on display. He can see the exact motion of my fingers as I swirl them over and around my button. Occasionally I even part the plump lips of my labia, pulling them back to show him how rosy pink they are inside. I show him the tight, dark tunnel he longs to enter. I can see that this excites him more than anything else and so I only do it right when he is on the very brink of orgasm. He looks and he shoots as if he were shooting his stuff straight into my hole.

Today when I got home, I discovered a special surprise, a gift to mark the one-month anniversary of our little routine. I unwrapped the tissue paper to find a small, pink vibrator just like the ones I'd seen in the window of the Museum of Sex – just the thing for my first gentle explorations. Pink for girls. Pink for pussies.

I gaze out again, surveying the rooms in my little dolls house. The Italian couple are entwined in post-coital sleep. The dominatrix new client is hard at work scrubbing her bathroom floor while she reclines upon him with a bottle of Dom Perignon.

An old couple watch television in the flat next-door to hers, oblivious to the display on the other side of the thick wall. The businesswoman is sitting down to dinner with the evening's companion, a sweet oriental.

Somewhere, in an apartment I cannot see, a baby is wailing. The other windows are in darkness at the moment. It is still early and most people stay out late in this district. The butcher's window, too, is dark. He must be on his way home from work. No matter. I shall wait for him. I smile because, though I have not yet bedded a man, I know just what to do to please him. When I finally decide to bring a boy home he will not see the coy shyness one would expect from a first-timer. What delights I will have in store for him!

Not just yet though. I am not yet ready. I have so much more to learn. For now I am content simply to watch my performing dolls every night as they go about their fascinating lives and to continue my strange relationship with the butcher – my pseudo-lover, my teacher, my watcher.

# For a Mistress

*Out of the depths of the darkness*
*She appears like a breath of light*
*To awaken my slumbering spirit*
*And restore me with freshness of sight*

*She stands, tall above me, in silence*
*A smile sparks her mouth and her eyes*
*'Tis filled with both kindness and cruelty*
*Which she needs not nor cares to disguise*

*Her lips and her whip grant me kisses*
*As she claims me in flesh and in soul*
*I am bound to her by her beauty*
*And her pleasure, alone, is my goal*

*Bedtime*

# Consequences

*I have always had a profound fascination with the Victorian era. We think of it as an era of high morality, when it was scandalous to show so much as an ankle, but I'm certain that as much debauchery went on in secret back then as it does today. The more we are told we shouldn't do something, the stronger the urge to do it. It is great fun to know we are breaking the rules.*

*Growing up in a time when caning in schools has been banned, I can only imagine what it would have been like to live back in Victorian times. I don't think I would ever have been able to sit down! Then again, perhaps I would have been better behaved. I have even started a small collection of Victorian clothing, courtesy of a friend of mine who shares my fascination. I adore dressing up in all the gear. I love the restriction of the ankle boots and rigid corset – there's nothing like a bit of self-bondage! The dresses with all their lace and frills are so feminine. I have two different kinds of drawers and both frame my bottom stunningly if I do say so myself. The first kind splits in the middle and can be pulled apart to reveal both cheeks and the second has a cute button-up flap which folds down. Back then it would have been far too much trouble for the ladies to remove their drawers from underneath their corsets, crinolines and outer-garments, and this way they could perform their ablutions more conveniently. The easily opened drawers must also have facilitated access should they want to disappear into their bedrooms for half an hour with a gentleman caller.*

*I find that, when I wear these clothes, though they show no flesh at all I feel sexier and more provocative than when I am clad in a skimpy bra and hotpants!*

*I think the main reason for my obsession with Victoriana is that it was the time when corporal punishment was at its height. It was commonplace both in schools and in the home. Wayward women were sent to Houses of Correction where they would be publicly chastised in front of an audience of onlookers. I love the idea of being punished purely for disciplinary reasons. This was not only acceptable but common practice in these times. Living as a young woman back then, I would have had no rights at all and everyone from my headmaster to the chambermaids would have had the right to spank me if they saw fit.*

*This is my Victorian diary, incorporating some of my deepest corporal punishment fantasies. I have combined the concepts of spanking for pleasure and genuine punishment designed to correct my behaviour and make me pay for my mistakes. If only I could build a time machine!*

Dearest Diary,

I have, as you know, always been more than a little nervous of my Aunt Estella. After careful reflection I believe it to be a combination of her abrupt, no-nonsense manner and her countenance, which always seems to be smiling at everyone else and frowning at me. I know she thinks me a 'wilful little miss' (her words!), but as far as I am concerned, my behaviour is none of her business. I detest the way she always scolds mother and father for being too lenient with me, especially where corporal punishment is concerned. I wish she would keep her nose out of where it is not wanted!

Most of the time I manage to avoid the horrid woman, shutting myself away in my bedroom whenever she takes it upon herself to come calling. But, awful as it is, I have just learned that mother and father have decided to depart on a trip to India! They have already booked their tickets on the liner and are due to leave as soon as the school term ends (less than a week). Despite my unending protests that I am old enough to look after myself, they have organised for me to stay with a relative during their absence. And who, dear diary, do you think they have chosen to entrust with my welfare?

Let me pause a moment whilst I describe her to you. Estella Charlotte Berkley is considerably taller than average, and though I loathe paying her a compliment, she has maintained a good figure despite her having seen the end of over forty summers. Her dress and manner are always pristine and respectable. Her fair hair seems to be forever entwined in a tight bun. Her high cheekbones and narrow ice-blue eyes give her an almost fox-like appearance. Her husband, my uncle, died so long ago that I cannot remember him and it is my belief he did it to escape her nagging.

She recently remarried but I have not yet met her new husband (as she did not feel I was old enough or well-behaved enough to attend their wedding!). Mother tells me he is a fine-looking gentleman and that he is a good ten years younger than she. Heaven knows what he sees in her! Of course I can tell no one but you, Diary, but it would not surprise me if he married her for her purse rather than her personality. Their large residence is tucked away in the small village of Bourton-on-the-Water in the Cotswolds and has belonged to our family for centuries.

I have only been there once, when I was very small, but I remember the apple orchard in which I spent most of my time. I shall leave you now as I am frightfully tired from arguing with mother and father and must get some rest.

Dearest Diary,

I bid farewell to mother and father this morning and have started on my way to Aunt Estella's. The journey is simply horrid. The carriage is old and the roads are full of stones. I ache from head to foot. It is nigh impossible to write without smudging the ink and so I will finish here.

Dearest Diary,

At long last I have arrived. As the carriage neared its destination I grew more and more tense. The house loomed before me and it seemed to have a cloud of ominous gloom hanging over it. It made me shudder. The carriage pulled up in front of the steps. One of Aunt Estella's maids was there to greet and attend to me. She said little but showed me through to my quarters, where I am now. The room is generous in size with white lace strung from the walls and a large quilted bed. I am quite pleased with the accommodation but shall be careful not to show this in front of Aunt Estella. It is true that I have to be here but I am determined to make sure Aunt Estella knows it is certainly not my choice of lodgings.

I believe I hear someone on the stairs. I shall write again presently.

Well, Aunt Estella has been here and left (in a mood, I might add). She walked straight into the room without even knocking. I only just hid you in time, dear Diary. I dread to think what she would have done had she found and read you! She greeted me with a formal nod as is her custom. She scrutinised me for what seemed like an age before she spoke.

'How do you find your quarters, child?' She never calls me by name! I stared back at her, defiantly.

'They shall have to do, I suppose,' I said with a haughty sniff. 'Though they are nothing like I am used to at home.'

'Quite the impudent little miss, are we not?' Aunt Estella snapped, raising an eyebrow. 'I think, girl, that the charms you present to the eye are more than adequate. However, a young lady cannot survive in society on her looks alone. Her outer beauty is worthless if not matched with a modest and agreeable disposition.'

'There is nothing wrong with my disposition,' I answered, trying with great difficulty to control my temper.

Aunt Estella pursed her lips. 'You've always had a will of your own. Such things are unbecoming in young ladies. It is the fault of your father. He has let you get away with far too much for far too long. But now you are under my roof, however, you shall follow my rules. I intend to make effective use of your stay here, and by the time I have finished with you, your behaviour will be impeccable. I am certain that you will find your time here most enlightening.'

For a moment, unless I am mistaken, there seemed to be a twinkle in her sapphire eyes. Something about the way she said 'enlightening' gave me an uneasy feeling in the pit of my stomach.

'Good day,' she nodded.

'Good day, aunt,' I replied dutifully, with an indignant toss of my chestnut hair. She carried herself with such dignity that it was impossible not to show her at least *some* respect. As much as I strove not to let her intimidate me, I could not help but breathe a sigh of relief as she left the room.

I must go now, Diary, as I still have a mountain of unpacking to attend to. Aunt Estella has not even sent one of the chambermaids to help!

Dearest Diary,

I have spent the last couple of days surveying every inch of the house and its gardens. I am thrilled that the orchard is still there and full of bright red apples, just like I remember it. I have befriended a few of the servants and am consequently learning many fascinating pieces of information about the household. One particular girl, a pretty thing named Catherine, has been an invaluable contact. She has shown me some of the secret passageways I can use to avoid Aunt Estella. I have also discovered that Aunt Estella's new husband, Sir Montgomery, is on one of his trips to London and is due home after lunch on Friday. He must present quite a picture, as Catherine got quite flustered when she spoke of him. I hope he is a more agreeable companion than Aunt Estella. I cannot wait until Friday!

Dearest Diary,

It is now Friday evening and I am so very excited. I have come straight to my room from dinner so I could write it all down before I forget. I shall start at the beginning.

After lunch there was still no sign of Sir Montgomery. I waited by the front steps for about half an hour, but this soon became rather tedious and so I decided to visit the orchard and pick some apples. I lifted my heavy skirts and climbed over the picket fence that surrounded it. I knew I should have used the gate but it was too hot to be ladylike today.

Then using the hem of my dress as a basket, I reached up and collected six or seven ripe, juicy apples. I found shelter from the sun in the shade of one of the trees, but even here I was unbearably hot and began to perspire. I was alone and so decided to remove my skirts. I used to do this quite often as a child and there was nobody around. With difficulty I undid the hooks and eyes at the back and wriggled out of the thick skirt-folds, then I relaxed against the tree trunk in nought but my chemise, corset and drawers, dozing contentedly. The sun beat down all around me and it was not long before my eyelids grew heavy and I could not resist the temptation to close them.

'Forgive my intrusion.'

I awoke suddenly and was greeted by the sight of a pair of shiny black boots in front of me. The second thing I noticed were my own legs, all bare apart from the stockings and drawers. Without even looking at my intruder I grabbed my skirts and dived behind the tree. I must have looked incredibly silly because Sir Montgomery (for it was he) burst out laughing. I was hurt and annoyed at being laughed at and by someone I had not yet met.

'I trust,' I remarked in my most condescending tone, fumbling as I hastily pulled on my crinoline and skirt, 'that it is not customary in this part of the country to sneak around and interrupt a lady whilst she takes her nap.'

'And I trust,' he replied with affected cordiality laced with mirth, 'that it is not customary in your part of the country for young ladies to lie around in their undergarments.'

I was simply bowled over by his impudence, so I took a deep breath, ready to let him have a piece of my mind and stepped out from behind the trunk. It was only then that I got my first glimpse of the stranger's face, and goodness, dear Diary! All of my annoyance drained away in an instant. His face was so handsome it would melt even Aunt Estella's icy heart and his figure would make any lady swoon. There was something about the way his inky brows flicked up at the outer edges that gave him a permanent expression of mischief.

'There now,' he said, smiling a most charming smile, 'that is much better. You must be Estella's naughty little niece. She has told me so much about you.'

I blushed, well aware of the kinds of things she would have said. He circled me slowly, looking me up and down. The look in his eyes made me uncomfortable, like a wolf sizing up its prey. He disappeared behind me and when he re-emerged in my periphery he was gleaming with sharp, white teeth.

'Well, Estella did not tell me what a pretty little thing you were. No, she most certainly kept *that* a secret. You are not the silly child she described. You have grown into quite a stunning young lady.'

I blushed even more deeply to hear such compliments. Never has a man spoken to me in such a way. I thought, for a moment, that I felt his hand patting the back of my skirt, but was not sure if I had imagined it. It would hardly have been appropriate behaviour for the husband of my Aunt.

'Well,' he added at last, 'I am pleased to make your acquaintance, my lady.' He bowed deeply and then offered me his arm, which I accepted graciously. He lowered his voice and leant so close to my ear that I could feel the heat of his breath. 'And do not fear. I shall not tell your aunt about your wayward behaviour this afternoon.'

I smiled as we walked back to the house, for even after this brief meeting I felt a huge affection for my new companion.

When Aunt Estella saw us walking through the front door, arm in arm, she did not look best pleased. I was sent immediately to my room to wash and prepare myself for dinner, and made a special effort to look as pretty as I possibly could. I put on my most sophisticated dress and tied blue satin ribbons in my hair.

Dinner itself was delicious, roasted pheasant with all the trimmings. Aunt Estella and Sir Montgomery sat at one end of the table and I at the other. Aunt took several opportunities to dish out a scolding, snapping at me for my lack of table manners and for being 'unsuitably overdressed'. But I did not mind any more, for every time she scolded, Sir Montgomery would glance at me when she was not looking and pull an absolutely hilarious face. And this caused me to giggle, bringing on even more scoldings!

'What that child needs is a good dose of proper discipline!' aunt exclaimed after my third or fourth outburst.

'I could not agree more, Estella,' her husband replied, and I nearly dropped my fork at such betrayal, but a sly wink from Sir Montgomery caused me to bite my tongue. 'You should have heard the cheek she gave me in the orchard just this afternoon.'

'That is the last straw,' cried Aunt Estella. 'I shall start her on a strict program of corporal punishment from tomorrow morning. I have heard that such measures are often adopted in the local schools. It will leave her sore and sorry enough to continue thinking about her behaviour throughout the rest of the day.'

'An excellent suggestion,' Sir Montgomery agreed, his face the picture of seriousness.

'Only why do you not let me take care of her myself? You are always so busy, dear Estella, and I am only too happy to give this little madam what she deserves. I believe I could correct her behaviour most effectively.'

Aunt Estella peered at him for a long time and then at me. I masked my joy, pretending to be very worried.

'Very well,' she said finally, 'but you are not to be lenient with her. She must learn how to behave before I soil my reputation by introducing her into society.'

My first disciplinary session is to commence tomorrow morning. I am certain that he acted in order to save me from Aunt Estella, but nonetheless I am to report to his study at nine o'clock. I cannot wait to see him again. I am certain that he is the most charming man in the entire world, even if he has an impudent streak. I must get my beauty sleep, dear Diary, if I am to rise so early. So I shall bid you an excited goodnight.

Dearest Diary,

I have so much to tell you and I want to write it all down before I forget. I asked that Catherine wake me early this morning (Aunt Estella has finally assigned her the duty of being my chambermaid) but I did not require her services. I was already awake as the first rays of sunlight squinted through the pane of my window. I breakfasted in my room. Aunt Estella always takes her morning ride at this time and so I knew we would be without interruption. We would probably just talk and laugh and eat teacakes until she returned. It was not until I had watched her dappled-grey mare disappear over the next hill that I did climb the stairs to Sir Montgomery's study.

'You're late,' he remarked sharply as I entered the room, and I fluttered my eyelids in the way I had seen the ladies do in male company.

'I am ever so sorry, sir,' I said in my sweetest voice, and waltzed over to the armchair, swaying my hips. I was about to take a seat when his voice stopped me.

'Did I say you could sit down?'

'Well, no sir, but I thought…'

'Then you thought wrong,' he interrupted. 'You thought I would let you off your disciplinary session, that I would just tell your aunt that I had chastised you? Unfortunately, my sweet, you do not get off that lightly. Your aunt wishes to inspect the marks when she returns.'

My heart leapt. Marks? Daddy has never so much as scolded me too sternly! What could I do, dear Diary? There was no way around it. I would simply have to let him punish me.

'Do not look so afraid, young lady. I am sure this will not be as bad as you imagine. Believe me, it would have been a lot worse if your aunt had taken your discipline into her own hands.' As he spoke, he got up from the desk and wandered over to me. His hand came to rest on my rear. This time there was no mistake.

'Estella tells me,' he said in a softer tone, 'that your Father never takes it upon himself to punish you. Am I to understand that your… if I may say so… beautiful little derriere is as much a virgin as your other chaste jewel? That you have never before been given a… sound… spanking?'

The enthusiastic way he said the word 'spanking' sent a chill right through my body. He punctuated the word with a deliberate squeeze to my rear and he spat out the consonants making it sound both terrifyingly harsh and exhilarating at the same time. I did my best to wriggle out of his clutches.

'W-well,' I stammered. 'F-father did spank me once or twice when I was a little younger.'

His eyes seemed to light up. He seemed delighted at my misfortune!

'Is that so?' he enquired with more interest than would seem necessary for the subject matter. 'Tell me how he spanked you. Did he put you over his knee or make you bend over and touch your pretty toes?'

My face was bright red. His words made me feel extremely uncomfortable; as did the strange, breathy way he spoke.

'Well, young lady? Answer me! I do not have all day to waste on you.'

I stared at the floor.

'He put me over his knee,' I mumbled. Why was Sir Montgomery treating me like this? He broke into a sly smile.

'I am glad to hear it,' he said, 'for that is exactly the way I intend to spank you. I certainly would not want to break such a family tradition.'

He leant close, gently stroking my silky hair, and then strolled over to the large Chippendale in the corner and sat himself down with the attitude of a king mounting his throne.

'Come here,' he commanded. I hesitated at first, but something about his look told me he was not to be disobeyed. He was, after all, master of the house, and could have me thrown out if he so chose. I shuffled over to him, coyly.

'Turn around,' he ordered. 'I wish to inspect my target before I attack it.'

I turned.

'Raise your skirts.'

Hesitantly I lifted them to my waist, giving him full view of my drawers. I was glad to be facing away from him and glad that he could not see the redness of my face. It was true he had seen me in that state before, but it was not the same as actually having to raise my dress and show him my underclothes deliberately.

Suddenly his hands grasped my buttocks, kneading and stroking them through the thin cotton. As you can imagine, dear Diary, I was too shocked to protest. I felt like a creature in the zoo! And to make matters worse, he actually spoke to me as he pinched and prodded my rear.

'You must understand that punishing young ladies is not a duty to be taken lightly. I must examine the constitution of the flesh in order to determine just how harsh a punishment you can take. I must assess the roundness of the curves to decide upon the most effective angle for my swing. I am something of a perfectionist, you see. Some have called me a connoisseur. I have spanked many deserving bottoms in my time, though I admit that I have not yet had the pleasure of spanking a girl as pretty as yourself.'

I could feel his shark-like grin pierce the air as he spoke.

'Excellent!' he said, finally moving away to seat himself on the large embroidered chair in the corner of the room. 'Now if you would be so kind as to place yourself across my lap.'

My first thought was to run from the room, but I feared

that would only land me in more trouble later on. Besides, my legs were as weak as jelly I barely managed to totter over to where he sat. I had no choice. I tried to force my knees to bend, but they buckled suddenly and I fell rather than 'placed' myself across the broad, muscular thighs I had admired so much previously.

He took one of my wrists and bent it securely behind my back in a vicelike grip. I found myself in a position from which no amount of kicking or struggling could set me free. I knew my rear end was rendered completely accessible, poking invitingly in the air. I have not been over father's knee for years so you can imagine, dear Diary, how I felt to be thrust into such a humiliating position!

By now I just wanted it to be over and done with, but he seemed to take pleasure in tormenting me, drawing it out for as long as he could.

'Now,' he said finally. 'This is for your impudence to me yesterday. You will find that I do not forget such outrageous behaviour in a hurry.'

I thanked Heaven that the material of my dress was quite thick. It should at least provide something of a barrier between my all-too-soft flesh and his all-too-firm hands. Glancing up, I saw Sir Montgomery's lips tighten as he raised one of them to his shoulder height.

'Face forward,' he barked. 'I want you to concentrate on what you are feeling.'

The pause seemed to last forever. The tick of the Grandfather clock against the wall seemed to dominate the room. I trembled, waiting for the sensation.

And then it came!

*Smack!*

The first expertly aimed spank landed on the seat of my

skirt, and I was shunted forward with the force, nearly toppling off his knee.

'This will not do!' he snapped. 'These skirts are providing too much protection. They shall have to be raised. Seeing as you seem to enjoy parading around in little but your bloomers, it seems only fitting that you receive your punishment in them.'

My mouth formed an 'O' as I felt each layer of my skirts and crinoline carefully raised, one by one, and arranged above my waist till my only defence was the thin material of the drawers.

It was then that I felt the first proper smack. For a moment all my senses went numb and then a searing sting speared into the right half of my nether regions like a lightening bolt. I let out a shocked whimper at the sensation and bit hard on my lower lip, ashamed of my own babyish response. Before I had time to collect myself a second burning kiss was planted on the other half, evening the effect. This time, with effort, I managed to receive the impact in silence.

More well targeted slaps landed with full force on my poor posterior. I felt my pelvis press against his sturdy legs. The buttons on his breeches were causing an awkward friction against the intimacy between my thighs. Oh, dear Diary, I pray as I write this that no one ever finds you! With much reluctance I realised that the humidity in this region had increased. My facial cheeks grew as red as those of my outraged posterior. I was thankful, at that moment, that my drawers safely hid my shame. He would not have been able to see the channel of sticky moisture down there. Then, as certain as if he had guessed my thoughts, came his next announcement.

'Well now, I do believe that these lovely drawers are

obstructing me from my duty. I am afraid that I shall have to pull them open. I want to be certain that this discipline is getting through to you. I shall deliver the remaining smacks directly onto your *bare* bottom.'

And to my utter horror, I felt him split the drawers in the centre and the coldness of the air caress my naked buttocks. I just wanted to hide. For the last ten years only my maids had seen the area that now confronted his gaze. I had thought as most young ladies did, that only my husband, when I chose one, would have the privilege of this view. Yet here I was, fully exposed to this man, practically a stranger! I could not bare it.

But Sir Montgomery seemed to ignore whatever anguish I was feeling and merely carried on determinedly with the task at hand.

'Just as I suspected!' he exclaimed. 'Your bottom is hardly even pink! I am sorry, young lady, but I shall have to remedy this at once or your aunt will be most displeased.'

Another rain of scalding smacks impressed their short, sharp message on my bottom. Ooooooh! How much more his wide palm stung when applied directly on the bare! Skin greeted skin with a resounding slap, a series of high-pitched squeals fought their way out of my mouth at this unexpected sensation, and against my navel I could feel a hardness growing in his breeches.

'Well, my proud young miss,' he said, 'how does it feel to be put over uncle's knee for a jolly good spanking, eh?'

I raised my head to catch a glimpse of his face, and I found that he was beaming from ear to ear and his eyes positively sparkled. He looked so handsome like this, almost majestic. He paused momentarily to admire his handiwork and massage my taut, velvety flesh with his palm. His nimble fingers probed into the valley between my buttocks, brushing lightly over my secret place. I was buried in mortification! I knew that he must have felt my wetness. It seemed to absorb his interest because he immediately raised the knee below my pelvic region so that my rear was raised even higher into the air. I felt my buttocks part slightly, giving him a better view of my wet private place. He remained in this position, placing his raised foot on a stool for support, and I gasped as I felt his fingers begin to trace around my intimacies. My bottom still burned from the spanking. I felt a bead of moisture form and drip down to form a puddle on his leg.

I wished I were anywhere but there. I wished that Aunt Estella had jolly well dished out the punishment herself. She would have just given me some swats and sent me on my way, sore and sorry. At least I would not have to face what I now felt. I could not help it. I was actually enjoying myself. The spanking had aroused strange sensations in me. It felt nice to be so close to him and have him administer to me so intimately. A funny feeling was building between my legs and I was powerless to stop it.

'So,' he grinned, 'it seems our naughty girl did not find her spanking to be a wholly nasty experience.'

I was too ashamed to speak. My wetness told all.

'Well, I think a few more smacks are required. We'd better not disappoint your aunt, had we?'

His hand began to descend again, awakening new fire in my buttocks. And this time his other hand let go of my arm and slid around my inner thigh and up to my rude place. I gasped, knowing I should pull away, but I could not bring myself to do so. As he spanked me his finger began to wriggle on the small mound of flesh that I had explored with my mirror not so long before on a rainy afternoon. He made small, vibrating movements just with the tips of his fingers, and it is difficult to describe the feeling he produced. It was like being tickled but in a nice way, tormented with pleasure. I know that makes little sense, dear Diary, but it is so difficult to describe the sensation. My whole body felt as though it was melting like wax.

Then suddenly, what felt like an explosion ran through my entire body and I shuddered. It was gorgeous! He pressed his whole palm over my place and I felt a flood of my own moisture seep into it. I began to cry. It was all so strange. Sir Montgomery ceased the spanking and began to rub my buttocks. He lifted me up and sat me on his knee.

'There there, young lady,' he smiled. 'You have been a very good girl. I just wanted to give you a nice little tickle, as a reward for being so good. We shan't mention this to your aunt. She thinks you are simply being disciplined.

'Run along now, and go and look in your mirror,' he said, his voice assuming a gentler tone. 'Your beautiful bottom has turned scarlet and I must say that it looks extremely fetching in this colour. That should leave Estella satisfied.'

I ran straight here to write everything down, dear Diary. It felt so bizarre but so positively scrumptious, and all I know is that I cannot wait until I am over my dear Uncle Monty's knee again!

Dearest Diary,

I was warned that Aunt Estella wished to inspect my marks, and inspect them she did. She was in my room just now and made me take off my dress completely and part my drawers. She laid her cold hands against my still warm flesh.

'Hmmph!' she grunted. 'Not as red as I would have left you, but not a complete waste of time, I see, and I sincerely hope we are now going to see a change in your behaviour, young lady.'

'Yes, auntie,' I answered in my most polite and ladylike tone, which obviously took her by surprise because she stared at me far longer than usual.

'We shall see,' she sneered as she turned to leave. 'But for now I think Montgomery ought to continue with your lessons.'

Ooh, that horrid old cow! How I detest her! But it is I who shall have the last laugh as she is merely granting me more time alone with the handsome Sir Montgomery. Perhaps I shall one day win his heart and steal him away from her clutches.

Dearest Diary,

Several weeks have passed since my last entry. I am afraid I have not had the time to write. Aunt Estella has put me on a regiment of household chores and, by the time I have completed them, I am too exhausted to even pick up a pen and ink.

My morning spankings continue and I look forward to them with great affection. They are the only time that I am alone with my sweetheart. Thankfully, Aunt Estella no longer makes her daily inspections. Sir Montgomery gave me an extra hard spanking during my tutorial (as he likes to refer to them) at the end of the first week. She seemed fairly satisfied with that and has failed to check up on me ever since.

Sir Montgomery constantly fills my dreams and my

daydreams. In my bed at night I have begun to tickle myself in the area he showed me, and discovered that I can achieve the same lovely explosion with my own two fingers. I believe I am developing quite a skill. In the hidden world of my imagination, my sweetheart tells me he can no longer stand to have Aunt Estella for a wife. He takes me by the hand and we elope. Of course he has never actually said anything of the sort to me in real life, but I am certain he cannot be happy with her. I am so much younger and prettier than she! He is bound to hold me in far greater esteem than that nasty old witch.

Dearest Diary,

A most peculiar thing happened during my tutorial today. I was really looking forward to it, and was already quite humid in my 'tickle' region before I even arrived at Sir Montgomery's room at the normal time of nine o'clock sharp. Montgomery was waiting for me in his chair as usual, so I skipped over to him ready to fling myself over his knee, but before I could lie myself down he stopped me.

'Just a moment, young lady,' he said, rather solemnly. I was taken aback by his tone. He did not seem angry, just serious. There was a rather odd look in his eyes, one I had not seen before. 'I think my little tutorials have done you the world of good. Not only has your behaviour improved but you have, in a very short space of time, begun to grow from a girl into a young woman.'

I positively beamed, bouncing up and down on my toes with pride.

'And so comes responsibility, young lady,' he went on, 'especially where men are concerned. In short, I believe the time has come to progress to the next stage of your schooling. Today you will prove to me that your behaviour is worthy of a well-behaved young lady. So, you will remove your outer garments and kneel in front of me.'

My eyebrows creased and I smirked a little. I was curious but uncertain what he wanted. Was it to be some new form of punishment? Would I like it? I hesitated.

'Now, now,' he questioned. 'Why such hesitation? You are fond of your uncle, are you not?'

I blushed and nodded.

'You do want to please me, don't you? I only want to give you a dose of my special medicine, the one I save for girls whom I hold in the greatest esteem. It will help you prove to me how exactly how much you have learned.'

That comment gave me the kick I needed, so I promptly knelt down in front of him. He parted his legs and pulled me into the gap between them. I felt myself blush even more, for the centre of his breeches was directly in front of my face. I had no idea where to look, so in a panic I shut my eyes.

'That's right, my dear,' he crooned. 'You just keep your eyes tightly closed. No peeking, now. That's very good... very good indeed...' I heard a rustle of material and the sound of hooks and eyes being undone.

'Now, open that pretty little mouth of yours,' I heard him say, and a moment after I obeyed there was a strange, rapid slapping sound and Sir Montgomery emitted a series of groans as though he were in pain. I was desperate to peek but remained obedient. The slapping sound grew faster and I could feel the heat of his body very close to my face. I could barely keep my eyes from opening, but then I felt a strong hand clapped over them and another grabbed my chin, forcing my mouth wider still, and suddenly a liquid filled my mouth and hit the back of my throat. It was warm and tasted like a mixture of salt and soap. I tried to close my mouth but the hands held it open like a vice. I coughed and spluttered and, for a moment, thought I was poisoned. I began to swoon and grabbed hold of Sir Montgomery's legs for support.

'There's a good girl,' my tutor murmured. 'Swallow all your medicine.'

I swallowed hard and the liquid slid down my throat, then there was a long exhalation of breath and the sound of hooks and eyes being done up.

'You may open your eyes again, my darling,' he said, somewhat wearily, I thought.

I did open my eyes, blinking a little as the light hit them. I felt dazed, not quite sure what had happened. I tried to stand but my legs were too wobbly. I looked up at Sir Montgomery, expecting to be greeted by his smiling face, but instead, to my dismay, he had collected his book from the table and was beginning to engross himself in its pages. I found my voice at last.

'Aren't... aren't you going to spank me and tickle me?' I asked.

'No,' he answered, not lifting his eyes from the page. 'You have finished your tutorial for today. You are dismissed.'

There was nothing more I could say. I was bursting with frustration and ran straight to my room. I placed my pillow in the centre of my bed and climbed over it. It was a poor substitute for my sweetheart's sturdy lap, but I lifted my skirts and unbuttoned my drawers. Raising my hand behind me I tried to bring it down with force, but it was no use. My poor hand hurt more than my bottom and so I gave up after three or four attempts. I grabbed you, dear Diary, and have been writing my frustrations down here ever since. I do hope my lessons will be back to normal tomorrow.

Dear Diary,

Five days have now passed and I have been too upset to write. My lessons continue to adhere to the new format. I have to kneel at Sir Montgomery's feet clad only in my drawers, corset and chemise, and close my eyes whilst he pours that horrid liquid down my throat. Afterwards I am promptly dismissed. I tried all sorts of tactics to earn myself the privilege of going over his knee again. I have shown him constant impudence and even deliberately spilled soup over his new jacket at dinner, but nothing works. He doesn't even tickle me any more. My heart is so heavy but I must continue as it is the only time I get alone with him.

Dear Diary,

I have so much to tell you. Please forgive my handwriting. I am forced to make this entry whilst lying on my bed as I simply cannot sit down.

I attended my tutorial this morning, kneeling with eyes closed to wait for the morning's 'medicine'. I heard the usual slapping sound growing faster, indicating that the liquid was about to arrive, when another sound pierced the room.

'What is the meaning of this?' A voice behind me made me jump and my eyes shot open. I gasped as I saw the exposed flesh of Sir Montgomery's manhood barely an inch from my face, but there was far greater cause for alarm than that.

Trembling, I turned slowly around to see the stern figure

of Aunt Estella framed in the doorway. Her countenance resembled an approaching storm and her fiery eyes shot darts of fury into the depths of my soul. She did not even look at her husband.

'Aunt Es-Estella,' I stammered. 'I... we...'

Sir Montgomery went immediately into action. He leapt up from the chair, knocking me to the floor as he did so.

'Thank God you are here, Estella,' he yelled. 'Now you can see for yourself just what kind of a niece you have. The little harlot tried to seduce me!'

My mouth dropped open but the shock and outrage transformed my words into a high-pitched squeak. Aunt Estella's face went positively purple! She marched over and caught me roughly by the hair. She dragged me out of the room and down the stairwell. I followed as best I could, half-staggering and half-crawling. I tried to pull my garments back on but Aunt Estella was marching too quickly.

'How dare you play the whore in this house!' she screamed. 'Thank God your father isn't here. Your behaviour would break his heart.'

At the foot of the stairs we encountered the butler, who seemed most intrigued by my state of undress though he tried not to show it.

'Fetch the trestle,' she snapped. 'And have all the servants meet here in the hall in one hour.' He nodded and set about his duties. Alarm flooded me. I had heard about the use of trestles in Houses of Correction, where wayward girls who hadn't had the privileges of our class were made to bend over and be punished for their wickedness.

Aunt Estella turned to me. 'As for you, little hussy, you can march straight out into the garden and make yourself a birch from the twigs of the tree by the coach house. You will report here with the finished implement in precisely one hour. And mind that you bind it well or you shall be forced to make another!'

My head was spinning like a top. What was I to do? I thought of running away, but where was I to go? (We are in the middle of nowhere). So I had no choice but to do as Aunt Estella had requested.

As I picked each birch twig, I could almost feel it biting into my tender flesh. I collected about twenty of them and took them back to the house. Catherine was kind enough to fetch me some string and then watched intently as I wound it round the base of the twigs, pulling them tightly together. My hands were shaking so much I could not tie the knot in place. The birch slipped from my fingers and fell to the floor, scattering the twigs all over the place.

Eventually I managed to bind them together securely. The seconds ticked by all too quickly and it was time to report to the hallway. My legs failed me and I had to lean on Catherine's arm for support as I made my way towards my awaiting punishment.

I could not believe my eyes when I arrived. All of the house's twenty-seven servants were seated around the edges of the hall. Some perched on the various levels of the staircase as though it were a Roman amphitheatre, some on the floor in front.

Their eyes turned to stare at me as I entered. A few looked upon me with sympathy but most held a great excitement at my predicament and at the proceedings. The wooden upside-down 'V' frame of the trestle had been erected in the centre of the spacious area in front of the staircase and it seemed to me like the executioner's gallows. Sir Montgomery was nowhere to be seen.

'Right,' snapped Aunt Estella, 'as you insist upon acting like a harlot then let us have you dressed like one. You can begin by removing your corset and chemise.'

I could not believe my ears. Surely she could not mean that I expose my breasts in front of the servants! I opened my mouth to protest but the look in her eye made me close it again. I tried to face away but could not as I was surrounded on all sides.

So reluctantly I undid the lace at the back of my corset and pulled it open. I slipped the chemise over my head. I could feel the eyes staring at my bare flesh all around me, taking in my soft breasts that none save my personal maids had ever witnessed. I tried to cover them with my hands, crossing my arms in front of me, over the pink nipples.

'Think yourself lucky, young lady,' Aunt Estella scowled. 'I did consider sending you to an actual House of Correction, but I cannot risk this scandal reaching the ears of my colleagues. Therefore you will be punished right here by me and in front of the rest of the household.'

'But, auntie,' I began, finding my voice at last.

'Silence!' she screamed. 'You are in enough trouble already. Take off your drawers and bend over the frame!'

'Aunt, no!' I screamed in a panic. 'What about my modesty!'

'Your modesty!' she exclaimed, and let rip with a laugh that held little amusement. 'You were hardly thinking about modesty in that room upstairs. The Devil has turned you into a loose woman. You must be stripped to the bare flesh so that I may thrash his influence out of you. Now take off your drawers!'

I hung my head to hide my tears and reached behind me to loosen each button. I slowly lowered the material and felt the eyes again, this time eagerly absorbing the sight of my bare bottom. If only I'd actually had my morning spankings over the last few weeks, I thought. That way my bottom might have become a little more resilient, but now it was as soft and vulnerable as ever.

Slowly I bent over the trestle. The bar of wood caught me across the pelvis and dug painfully into my hipbone. My hands reached down the other side to grab hold of the frame at the bottom so I stood on tiptoe with my slim body tilted into a sharp angle.

I could see nothing but the crimson Indian carpet, but I could hear Aunt Estella pacing up and down behind me like a palace guard. She swiped the birch a few times, allowing it to whistle through the air for effect. The breeze it created reached my buttocks and the coolness delved between the cheeks. I knew they must be parted slightly, allowing everyone behind me a splendid view of my most intimate places. But I no longer cared about immodesty. All I could concentrate on was the anticipation of the pain I was about to receive.

'Legs straight!' Aunt Estella demanded. 'Rear out! Make it invite the attention of the birch! That's it. Now, you are going to receive twenty strokes. And if you dare to move an inch from that position you shall earn yourself another ten. Do I make myself clear?'

'Yes, auntie,' I choked.

I screwed up my face and felt my buttocks twinge expectantly. Aunt Estella waited and my tension increased with every second.

Then, *swisshh-whaaackk!*

The birch exploded across both my buttocks making the flesh bounce. The impact took me by surprise. My hips cut into the wood and I danced from one foot to the other.

'Stand still, I say!' she warned. 'That's another ten. You are up to thirty now, young lady.'

My clumsiness was rewarded by an even fiercer stroke. It took every fibre of my will to remain in place, but I succeeded. Each stroke seemed to increase in intensity. I am certain Aunt Estella kept hitting harder and harder to force me into disobeying her again. Stubbornly I made it to fifteen, but the sixteenth stroke was so utterly ferocious that I stood straight up and hopped around the room pressing my hands to my burning bottom. The heat from it was so intense I could barely hold my palms to the skin.

Aunt marched over to me, and as I scrambled to avoid her I slipped and fell flat on my front with my legs spread wide behind me. A few of the better-brought-up ladies averted their eyes, but the rest of the household burst out in gales of laughter. My pride stung as much as my poor bottom. How could I ever show my face around the house again?

Aunt caught hold of me and literally flung me back over the trestle. All sense of counting was forgotten. Aunt Estella's arm descended in a steady rhythm. The birch bit and bit and bit, proving its effectiveness with every strike. I could see splinters of wood breaking off and accumulating on the carpet each time the birch landed. My proud breasts heaved against the wooden frame. My bottom jerked and bobbed, desperately trying to escape the painful onslaught, but Aunt Estella was merciless in her resolve.

'Pleeease, Aunt Estella,' I sobbed. 'I can't taaaake any more. I'm truuuly sorry for my behaviour. I will be better in future. I swear in the name of God.'

She got in a couple more excruciating wallops and then

cast the birch to the floor. My blistered bottom was frightfully ablaze. I feebly struggled to my feet.

'Get out of my sight!' Aunt Estella screeched, and she did not need to tell me twice. I didn't even collect my clothes but scampered up those stairs as naked as the day I was born, pushing grinning servants out of the way as I ran.

I reached my room, still shaking, and collapsed on my bed, crying tears of sorrow, pain, shame and fury into my pillow. I cried until I had no tears left and then skulked over to my looking glass. My reflection showed that my swollen hemispheres were decorated with tiny scarlet flecks where the scalding ends of the birch had left their reminders of my punishment.

It seems unfair that my previously flawless bottom has paid the price for my misdemeanours. Already the sting is transforming into a smarting glow all over. A deep, purple hue is growing beneath the surface, spoiling the pretty pinkness of the skin.

Dear Diary,

It is now morning and I arise with a fresh joy in my heart. There are but a few pages left in you, Diary, but I am glad I am able to record the events of last night.

As you know, I was lying facedown on my bed sulking over the blistering agony in my nether regions, when I heard a knock at the door and immediately thought it was Aunt Estella come to give me another lecture. To my relief, however, it was Catherine who entered the room. I expected her to laugh at my sorry state but she simply smiled. Her expression was a mixture of pity and curiosity.

'Please, miss,' she asked coyly, 'will you let me administer to your wounds?'

I looked into her brown eyes and saw no trace of mockery in them. I nodded. She scurried over to the cabinet, took out a small pink jar, and came to kneel beside me on the bed. Then dipping her fingers into the cold cream, she massaged the soothing mixture into the appropriate areas. I winced a little at first, but it felt lovely.

'You poor thing,' she whispered. 'It was naughty of you to allow yourself to be seduced, but she needn't have treated you in such a way.

'I hope you do not mind me saying this, miss, but you did look very beautiful, even when you were bent over being birched.'

I smiled bashfully. 'But look at my poor bottom now,' I moaned. 'The sight is quite shocking!'

'If I may say so, miss, I do not agree,' she countered gently. 'I think that the bruising takes nothing away from the prettiness of your bottom. It is as if the marks make it somehow... nobler, like a war hero emerging triumphantly with the fierce scars of battle. And I do believe that the attack it has suffered only adds to its beauty.'

Her fingers worked their magic with attentive and loving care. Eventually the throbbing subsided and my bottom felt tender and warm. I was actually able to sit upon it, lowering myself as delicately as possibly onto the bed.

'Miss, I have a confession to make,' she said, looking away. 'During your disciplinary sessions with Sir Montgomery, I... I often peeked through the keyhole.' She paused a moment, clearly observing my reaction to such an admission.

'The sight stirred strange feelings in me,' she went on, when she assessed it safe to do so. 'I do hope you don't mind me saying this, but... I wished that I were the one giving you the spanking. Even from the door I could see how excited it made you and I longed to be the one who made you so excited... I'm sorry... I shall leave you now.'

'No, don't go,' I said hastily. 'Please, stay with me.'

'Very well, miss,' she said cautiously, and then her mouth broke into a smile and her eyes narrowed slightly. 'But it is a little chilly out here. May I not hop in the bed there beside you?'

I knew how inappropriate her suggestion was, but at that moment there was nothing I wanted more.

I lay perfectly still for some time, feeling awkward and not daring to move. Then I felt her hands reach over and stroke the flesh of my stomach. She moved closer so that our whole bodies touched.

'You liked Sir Montgomery, didn't you?' she whispered in my ear.

'I... I used to,' I answered.

'But he never kissed you, did he?'

'Well, no, not exactly,' I admitted.

'I would have kissed you if I was he,' she told me. 'I would have kissed you the way the French people do. Would you like me to show you how that is?'

I knew I should be repulsed by the suggestion, but I wasn't.

'Yes, please,' I whispered tentatively. 'I believe I would like that very much.'

Oh, dear Diary, how we kissed! We kissed for hours, her tongue darting into my mouth and mine into hers. The moistness grew between my thighs again. I took hold of her hand and guided it down to my 'tickle' place. She ran her fingers over it eagerly and the feeling of her soft skin was so much nicer than it ever was with Sir Montgomery. After all, her tickle place is the same as mine, so it seems only natural that she understands its pleasures so much more than a man would.

I heard footsteps approach, and just in time Catherine dived under the covers of my bed and pressed herself close to me so that our bodies made a single shape beneath the quilt. The door opened and Sir Montgomery appeared. He looked pale and scruffy and there were dark circles beneath his eyes. Aunt Estella must have given him quite a talking to. I wondered how I could have ever considered him handsome. He paused for a long time before he spoke, as if he were summoning the courage.

'I am sorry for what happened,' he said at last. 'I had no choice. I have not put up with Estella for this long to have her turn around and write me out of her will now. But do not worry, my precious. We will find another way of getting together to continue our little sessions.'

I raised my head to meet his eyes directly.

'I do not think that will be necessary,' I announced, in my most determined manner. 'Both you and Aunt Estella shall see a great change in my behaviour from now on. I am afraid that I shall no longer have any need of *your* services, sir.'

As he meekly turned and left, without another word, he seemed more pitiful than a puppy scolded for chewing its owner's slippers, and the moment the door closed I threw back the covers and the two of us burst into a fit of giggles. I cuddled Catherine and she cuddled me back. And it felt all the nicer for being forbidden.

I slid my fingers over her silky flesh, enjoying the fact that it felt like mine. We stayed in the warmth of each other's arms all night, and in the morning she kissed me and left to fulfil her duties, promising to return soon.

I will have to watch my behaviour during the day, but what of that? I can easily be prim and proper in society's company, biding my time until the evening. Then, in the cosy darkness of her room and mine, I shall be far more naughty than Aunt Estella could ever imagine!

*Resignation*

# The Marionette

*This fantasy was initially inspired by a suspension bondage demonstration given by a wonderful lady known as Fetish Diva Midori. I originally worked with her in New York and absolutely loved the experience. She whispered sensual fantasies in my ear as she tied me and the photographs were taken. Naturally, I was thrilled when she emailed me to ask if I would like to be suspended during a demonstration she was to give in London.*

*Midori is an amazing person. She is intelligent, sexy and witty. She is also an expert in Japanese rope bondage. Listening to her voice is like inhaling the aroma of rich coffee. It was an honour to be her model and her submissive. She introduced me to the audience and told them what an obedient and delightful sub I was. I blushed and bowed my head.*

*She bound my hands tightly behind my back and then wove a beautiful harness over my torso and under my crotch. She attached the ropes around my breasts to a wooden frame and hoisted me up so that I had no option but to stand on tiptoe. She took advantage of my flexibility as a ballerina to raise my right leg behind me. The left followed shortly after so that I was suspended horizontally above the floor. The audience applauded appreciatively but Midori had only just begun to have fun.*

*I was moved onto my side and then flipped onto my back. She next tied my ankles together and loosened the ropes around my waist and chest so that I hung upside down. She kept moving my position in the air, tying a rope here and untying another there until I appeared to be performing an ever-changing tableau of graceful, balletic poses. It must have looked incredibly beautiful. It certainly felt so.*

*While I dangled there I was put in mind of a puppet, helpless, held up only by her strings and subject to the will of the puppeteer. I usually remain fairly professional during my work, but on this occasion I lost myself in the fantasy, moving into an almost trancelike state of pleasure. I cleared my mind completely and simply enjoyed the sensation of floating in someone else's control. I was totally dehumanised, transformed into a mere object of service.*

*This form of sexual fulfilment is deeply psychological. This idea lies at the core of my submission. I still think it is one of the most beautiful fantasies of all.*

She felt nothing. After all, puppets do not feel. Their smooth, flawless, wooden faces are not masks designed to hide a multitude of thoughts, ideas and terrors. Such human burdens are far beneath them. A smile cannot spoil the perfect roundness of their lips, nor do tears smudge the delicately painted eyes. In becoming the marionette she had cast off any soul within her and passed everything into the hands of the puppet master. He would do the thinking for her now; make her decisions, control her actions.

He had been her lover once, the first to take her to bed and show her all the clandestine pleasures she had only ever imagined. Every evening he would take his candlestick in one hand and her arm in the other and lead her all the way up the wooden stairs to his bedroom. There, wrapped in each other's warmth, they would commence their special lovers' games. She would explore his body and her own. She would take his manhood in her learning lips as he nuzzled into delicate folds at the entrance to her womb, awakening her pleasure with a spit-soaked tongue.

But it was the daytime that she treasured most of all. She would perch for hours on the tall stool in the corner of his workshop, content to simply watch him work. She loved the smell of the paint and timber. She loved to see each puppet begin to take shape, its parts carved from a solid block of wood by his skilful hands and then polished to an almost impossible smoothness. The parts were then intricately assembled, threaded together to form a movable body.

The painting of the faces was the most compelling part of all. Each one was so eerily lifelike that witnessing its creation was like watching the miracle of a new baby's birth.

He rarely spoke to her as he worked. His concentration was so deep, especially when each puppet neared its completion, that he would sometimes forget she was there and call out to her to come and see the finished doll.

The completed marionettes were sold to puppeteers all over the world. His reputation for the perfection of his products was unmatched. He would keep the very best dolls for himself. He never knew which ones would take his fancy until he had added the final touches. Only at that ultimate stage would he discover something about that particular doll that caused him to place it with care in his ancient, leather trunk, rather than displaying it on his shop shelf to be sold to an eager customer.

Sometimes he would take his little collection out of their boxes and put on a private show just for her. She would fall under their magic, staring with childlike delight as his talented hands breathed life into them; their bodies, otherwise as dead as the wood they were made from, suddenly became animated under his command. He would make them dance, leaping about like little ballerinas, twirling and spinning on their strings. Sometimes, with a wicked smile, he would make them re-enact the secret things that he did to her in his bedroom after dark. At the end he would make them bow deeply before locking them away again in his trunk.

It was obvious from the delight on her face that she adored these little shows, but the puppet master could never have guessed how deep their effect on her was. He never dreamed that, while she sat mesmerised by the scene before her, her imagination began to run wild, filling her with questions and intense desires. What would it be like to be one of her lover's immaculate marionettes, to be completely at the mercy of his commands? To be only granted life at his will and by his hand? Surely that must be the most noble of existences! She thought how blissful their lives must be, free from the daily worries of decision making and all the tyrannies of the human world, waiting silently in their boxes until they could be brought out and put to service.

She became increasingly fixated with the idea. She would lie awake at night thinking about it, nestled in her lover's arms as he slept. She would smile at the ridiculousness of her dream. She saw herself as a strange reverse-Pinocchio. The puppet's sole wish had been to become a real live boy and she, handed the gift of humanity on a platter, longed to be a lifeless wooden marionette.

But why was the thought so bizarre? She worshipped the puppet master and wanted to be his completely. So great was her love that she wanted to give him not only her body, but also her will. What was so odd about that?

One night, in the cosy, naked stillness after their lovemaking, she confessed her desire to him. She had expected him to laugh and to call her a foolish child, but his face remained serious. He stared at her with the same deep concentration that she had seen in him so often as he painted his puppets. His eyes seemed to take in every detail of her face, the degree of curvature in her dark lashes, the precise shade of green in her iris, the configuration of her lips. The pale blue moonlight through the window made his grave face seem as though it were made of stone. It was like a mask of permanent seriousness. No emotion, if he felt any, could penetrate through to show on its surface. The look frightened her. It was as though he were no longer looking at a human being but an object with no more feeling than the blocks of wood from which he carved his creations.

After a long time he rose and walked away from her, out of the room. Her panic rose. Had she offended him? Had her unnatural desires driven him off? She waited in the dimly lit room, and eventually she heard his footstep on the stairs once more. His form appeared in the doorway. In his hand he carried a bamboo rattan of about a yard in length and some rope made from hemp that he must have retrieved from the shelves in his workshop. He advanced towards her with steady, deliberate tread. He said nothing.

Seizing her wrist, he dragged her up to kneel against the wooden headboard. At either side of it was a lion's head. He had carved them many years ago when he made the bed. He bound each of her wrists to the sculptures, winding the rope around the wrist several times before knotting it so hard it pinched her skin. Her outspread arms forced her face forward so that her cheek rested against the flat board of the frame. She tried to look back at him but could not turn her head more than a few inches.

Suddenly she felt the rattan sting her naked buttocks. She screamed, not understanding what she had said to invite such treatment. It swiped her again, bringing tears to her eyes, which threatened to escape. Had she angered him? Or was he putting her through some kind of test? If he was then she wanted to prove herself. She gritted her teeth and squeezed her eyes shut, trying to block out the pain. The rod fell another four times, the last one cutting across the narrow flesh just beneath her shoulder blades. It was no use. She could not hold back her tears. The two lions watched as they spilled from her eyes and ran down the smooth bed-head to soak the sheets beneath. She was ashamed of them, ashamed of her own weakness.

'Look at you,' he yelled, 'stained with human tears. Allowing emotion to debase you. My puppets are perfect, unmarred by such human imperfections. How can you aspire to being one of them when tears leap from your eyes the minute you are struck?'

'Train me then,' she cried. 'Improve me. Teach me to be as free from emotion as wood.'

He stood in silence, reading her expression, and at last he spoke.

'You will be my property. You will have no rights of your own, no thoughts. You will not wear clothes. Such things belong in the human world. What is more, you cannot expect to become a puppet straight away. You must first prove yourself worthy and capable. Is this what you desire? Think carefully, my child. If you decide then this decision will be your last.'

She paused for a moment, not wanting him to think she

had taken the choice lightly, but there was never a doubt in her mind.

'Yes,' she murmured. 'I shall be yours. Use me as you will.'

And thus their life continued. She began to serve him. Day by day he transformed her into different objects that he required. Some days she would be a writing desk, tilted at an angle from the waist as he placed the paper carefully onto her back. She would have to remain in this position, not moving an inch as he wrote his letters or went through the sums of his accounts.

Some days he would make her lie upon his workshop bench, actually becoming his work surface for the afternoon, resting all the parts of his creation on her breasts, belly and thighs as he assembled them.

In the evenings she would often become his footstool, kneeling with head bowed as he relaxed in his armchair reading, ankles resting their full weight on her shoulders.

She was not permitted to bed with him any more unless he desired her presence. She would sleep on the Indian rug in the corner of the room until morning. Gradually she became used to the hardness of the floor and could sleep through the night quite comfortably.

It was difficult at first. Her mind was still clouded by human thought. This old habit could not be dropped in an instant. Often he would beat her, daring her to cry. The dreaded rattan would descend in challenge against her fragility. When he struck her a little harder than her soft flesh could take, she would cry out. Unwanted tears would flow from her eyes and he would hurl down the rod in frustration.

But, as with everything, she began to improve with practice. Her limits extended. She learned to curb her wailing and each time there were fewer and fewer tears.

One evening he fetched a stick of butter from the larder and led her into the bedroom. She wondered what new task she would be set this evening. Forcing her down on all fours on the rug, he pushed her front half down until her breasts touched the floor and her rear remained high in the air. Taking some rope, he secured her hands behind her back, elbows bent at right angles and each hand grasping the opposite elbow. He went to the cupboard and took out a large candle. The wick was new. He lit it and then held the candle beneath the butter to soften it.

Dipping his fingers in the butter, he began to smooth it over the soft pink flesh around her anus. He dipped his forefinger inside, smoothing the oily butter into her. She winced slightly. In all their previous bedroom frolics he had never until now penetrated this most intimate of all her body's places.

When he was satisfied her skin was ready, he placed the candle over the tight asterisk and pushed. The agony as the shaft of wax slid inside her made her dizzy and she feared for a moment she would faint. She tried to switch her mind off what was happening, but the pain was incredible.

At last she managed to blank her mind, taking a deep breath and relaxing her body as much as she could. He eased the candlestick deeper, and when the waxen pillar was buried by three inches, he put his hand on the back of her head as he did when he intended her not to move, and climbed into bed with his book.

She knew she must keep absolutely still lest the flame flicker and disturb his reading. She denied her very bowels the reflex of pushing out this foreign object. She felt the first drops of wax slide down the candle and onto the sensitive skin. Every instinct tried to make her body jolt, but she fought them and did not budge.

Slowly the wax melted and dripped down onto her bare, vulnerable flesh. The pool of wax spread out over itself, stuck to her skin and hardened. An hour passed and she did not move. The candle burned right down until it almost extinguished itself in its own pool of liquid wax. Still she remained as steadfast as stone, until at last it was time.

Her lover put down his book and moved to his little candleholder.

'My darling,' he whispered as he knelt down to blow out the candle, 'I think you are ready for your grand performance.'

He had groomed her with obsessive care. The white greasepaint covering her face made it appear as though she were sculpted from purest alabaster. Her blood-red lips and charcoal eyes with the long caterpillar lashes were painted with symmetrical perfection. Her chestnut tresses, normally an unruly mane about her head, were tamed into ringlet curls and held in place on either side of her head with blue ribbons. Two rosy suns were painted on her cheeks, and finally, a tiny teardrop was drawn below her right eye as if to mock the tears she could not shed.

Her dress was of the purest white lace, held tight to her waist by a satin corset and on her feet, a brand new pair of ballet points he'd ordered for her from Russia.

She waited in the darkness behind the thick velvet curtain, the barrier between ordinary life and fantasy, though the question of which side is the more real is left to the realm of philosophers. The rope-strings held her as securely as a snare. They were firmly attached to her various limbs and joints, and beneath her costume three strong ropes swept down in a V-shape under her crotch.

The other ends of the strings reached upwards to a giant controller frame high above the stage. It had taken him months to make the controller, resizing every piece to scale so that her body could be twisted and bent like his puppets in whichever direction he wished. It swung from the roof and could be tilted this way and that so he could work it easily without having to bear her weight. A pulley system could raise it or lower it. He would dictate her every movement through her strings. She could not so much as scratch her nose unless the puppet master deemed it so.

She closed her eyes. She should have been aflutter with the nerves inherent in stage performance, and yet she could not remember ever in her life feeling such a deep sense of relaxation. It was as if all her worries and concerns had been lassoed as tightly as her limbs and lifted away from her mind.

It was time. The puppet master, high in the gods, relaxed the ropes to allow her body to gently slump to the floor, motionless, as though she were asleep. In the tiny space between the base of the curtain and the stage boards she could see the houselights dimming and hear the excited babble of the audience fall to anticipatory hush, as if the theatre itself had sucked the words from their mouths.

Slowly the curtain began to rise. A single spotlight picked out her lifeless form in the centre of the black stage. Gradually the puppet master tilted one end of the giant controller. The rope became taut and a limp hand was raised high in the air. The marionette was pulled into a sitting position, her curls flopping forward over her bowed head. The strings were pulled again and the ones supporting her crotch lifted her until she stood on highest tiptoe. Her head was raised upright so she could stare, with a rigid beauty, at the audience.

The puppet master hoisted her arms into the fifth ballet position above her head, and then her leg was slowly lifted until it was just as high and she balanced on one foot. She wobbled for a second but the halter beneath her groin ensured she would not fall. She felt completely safe, as though a giant hand held her in its palm.

The orchestra began to play, first the strings with their smooth, melancholic strains followed by the pregnant groans of the accordion. The stage lights were raised fully. The stark white of her costume against the black of the backdrop made her a silhouette in reverse. She began to dance, as if the music wove a spell on her, enchanting her body. The strings worked up and down making her twirl on her points while her arms circled in sweeping movements around her. Her knee was lifted to her chest and then the rest of the leg extended elegantly in front of her. She arched backwards until she could almost touch the floor behind her, and then was hoisted back to an upright position.

The dance continued. At times she felt her own will fighting back, urging her to move this way or that, but every time she tried to follow it the puppet master wrenched her ropes and steered her in the direction he chose.

Suddenly the puppet master jerked the controller and the puppet leapt high into the air in a graceful arabesque. The ropes caught her and left her spinning in mid-air. For a second she imagined she was Arachne, the impudent girl who challenged the jealous goddess, Minerva, to a weaving contest and was turned into a spider as punishment for her victory.

The ropes bit into her, chaffing her delicate skin. The controller jerked on the ropes again and lifted her feet so that they were level with her head. She was swung horizontally above the stage like a lady in a magician's levitation act. She let the sling of rope take the full weight of her head. She cleared her mind and closed her eyes. She could have floated in this way forever but this was not the will of her master. Gradually he pulled on the ropes that controlled the top half of her body. She was tilted into a vertical position so that all the weight fell to the ropes that held her arms and crotch, and the pulley system hoisted her whole body until it was about ten feet off the stage. The position was agonising, and for a moment she felt as though she were being crucified. She fixed her lips in place determinedly and did not struggle. Tears began to well but she refused to let them defeat her. This was what she had wanted, to be wholly in her master's control. She convinced herself that here, in his power, she was as strong as a mighty oak.

As she hung there the pain subsided and she began to feel all sensation draining from her body. She could no longer feel it. She was not certain that she had a body any more. Perhaps she was simply a mind, floating freely in the air. The audience, the theatre, even the puppet master all melted away.

The puppet master let her hang there, allowing the audience to absorb and appreciate the beauty of the sight before them. She appeared like an angel, hovering above the stage, arms outspread like wings.

At last he took a razor-sharp knife from his coat pocket and leant over to cut one of the strings. The split second the knife sliced through it the puppet's left hand flopped at the elbow. The knife sliced again and her hand fell to her side. She did not move or lift her head. Another two strings were severed and this time her right hand joined its companion at her side. The strings attached to the wrists and elbows dangled below.

But the puppeteer was not yet finished. Soon the ropes attached to her knees and ankles were also hanging below her, and now it was only the ropes beneath her crotch that supported her. They pulled tightly, and in the hazy, semi-conscious cocoon in which her mind now dwelt, she wondered if they would slice her in two. They did not.

Gradually the puppet master lowered her so that her feet touched the stage once more, and there was a sharp prickling sensation as the blood raced into them. And it had been so lovely to feel nothing!

The puppet master reached out and cut the final ropes and his puppet collapsed onto the stage again, where she finished the performance as she had started it – a lifeless doll.

After the applause had died down, the curtains had been lowered, and the audience returned to their own private realities, the puppet master released his marionette from her strings. Slinging her over his shoulder, he took her home and folded her neatly away in his ancient trunk. She lay there, curled up in the dark, feeling the peace of an infant in its mother's womb, and as she lay her body began to change. No more did heavy bones form its internal foundation. Instead thin, sturdy string linked each section of her limbs, torso and neck. Her skin lost its vulnerable softness, hardening to become smooth and finely shaped. Her face, too, lost the last human traces of emotion to become forever perfect, forever young and forever beautiful. Though her lips could not smile, she was happier and than she had ever been before. The marionette closed its wooden eyes and waited patiently until it could next be of service.

# Worship

*Okay, I admit it. When I first began to discover the world of Internet chatrooms and found my way into a 'BDSM Dungeon', I acquired a Cyber-Mistress. Her name was Mistress Whiteheat and I would chat to her every night, typing away on my computer while my parents sat, unsuspecting, in front of the television downstairs. It is amazing what an erotic experience it was, given that we had nothing to arouse each other with except for words on a screen. It was from her that I received my first slave training.*

*Every day she would set me a new task. Sometimes she would make me masturbate with her, in front of the computer, typing with sticky fingers to let her know that I had cum for her.*

*Once, when she was dissatisfied with me, she made me place slices of jalapeno pepper over my nipples. They burned for about three hours! I know I could have simply told her that I had done so, but it wouldn't be the same. Besides, she seemed to know when I was lying. It amazes me now that I gave such constant devotion to a name on a screen, but it is easy to get swept up in such a theatrical, cosy fantasy world. A person can be who they want to be without the judgement of first impressions based on looks. On the Internet we are all beautiful, charming and gallant.*

*In this story I wanted to show you a glimpse of the little world we built, a world of sensuality and chivalry. Perhaps it was because I was young and impressionable but, at the time, I worshipped her.*

A spark of light as a match is struck. The blaze flares for a second, illuminating the delicate hand which holds it, then shrinks to a fragile flame. From my corner I watch the pinpoint of light travel to kiss the candle, endowing it with light and warmth. As the glow seeps into the room I see her! My goddess!

She claims to be mortal, but no. Beauty such as hers was never meant for this world. The flame lends her nothing for her own brightness makes it grow pale with jealousy. I avert my eyes from her radiance, my face burning with shame that I did dare to look at her. What right is it of mine to cast my undeserving eyes on a goddess? I am no more worthy simply because I belong to the same fair sex as she. My own guilt punishes me far more than her whip ever could. And yet, her beauty corrupts me and steals my will so that I am forced to look again. Her eyes catch mine for an instant and her mouth breaks into a smile. She laughs at my insolence.

'Forgive me, Mistress,' I whisper, kneeling at once at her feet, 'but it is by thy splendour that I am made bold.'

Her hand comes to rest on my head. I close my eyes and tremble, expecting her rage, knowing that at any moment the storm will erupt and its lightening strike my foolishness. But it does not.

'You have much to learn, little one.' Her voice wraps me in velvet.

I crave, with all my being, to look on her again, but this time I do not dare. I want to touch her. I want to caress her sublime frame and know her beauty is real, that she is not some muse conjured by my own desires to torment me.

She withdraws her hand and walks gracefully over to

the cabinet. She takes a glass from its resting place and fills it with rich, crimson wine. The scent of it plays on my nostrils and I grow dizzy.

'Come to me, child,' she entices.

I would not disobey even if I had the power or the courage to do so. She takes a small but exquisitely sharp knife from the cabinet. I feel no fear; I am her property and she may treat me as she pleases.

She takes my hand, pricking the forefinger with the blade. There is a second of pain but it is sweet pain as it is my goddess who causes it. A scarlet bead of blood forms over the wound. She holds it over the glass and it falls, mingling with the wine.

*One for the mistress.*

She squeezes gently to encourage another drop. My very blood obeys her.

*One for the slave.*

She squeezes again and a third drop leaps to the glass at her bidding.

*One for the relationship they build together.*

She swirls the liquid, making it glitter in the candlelight, and drinks. Only when her own thirst is satisfied does she offer me the glass. She holds it to my lips and tilts it so that the sweet liquor slides onto my tongue and down my throat. Its effects are immediate. My head swims in bliss. She entwines her fingers in the soft dark curls of my pubic hair and leads me to her ornate chaise longue. I kneel in my place at the foot of it.

She walks over to her chest. The carved ivory container is full of mysteries that I am not permitted to see. It holds the implements of control and punishment that she amuses herself by testing on me from time to time.

Today she brings out two ropes of deepest burgundy,

one about a half an inch thick and the other slightly finer. She unwinds them methodically as she approaches me. My sex starts to moisten as soon as I glimpse the rope. The very sight of it makes my cunt drool in an almost Pavlovian reaction. I begin to wonder how she will make use of me today. In which position will she choose to bind me? I know I am never more beautiful to her than when I am bound.

She begins with my feet, harnessing them together, side-by-side, the thin rope crisscrossing them like a fisherman's net. She winds the silky rope between each toe and pulls it taut around the heel. The rope tickles my feet and I bite my lip to prevent myself from flinching or giggling.

When she is satisfied the ropes are secure, she weaves a string of tiny pearls into them. Like most ladies, she loves to decorate her work.

She orders me to sit up straight and then begins to slide the thicker rope over my shoulders and around my lower back. It zigzags over my torso in a tight harness. She pushes down onto my stomach. The cold slate floor bites into my nipples as my breasts are crushed against it. She threads the rope down between my legs. I spread them for her, showing her my arousal. Rolling me onto my back, she collects the rope up and knots it twice so that the double knot is positioned directly over my clitoris. She parts the rope and twists it around my waist.

'Now, how tightly shall I tie you?' she whispers teasingly. 'Shall I allow you the pleasure of the ropes?'

To my delight she pulls it taut. The knot presses into my hungry clit and I squirm under the pressure. I squeeze my thighs together and arch my back slightly, pulling the rope tighter still so that it rubs firmly against me. I cannot help murmuring my delight as she rolls me over again.

She takes both my arms and stretches them behind me. She binds them tightly at the elbows and wrists. I loosen my body, allowing it to become like a floppy rag doll, easy for her to manipulate. Grabbing my pointed feet she bends my legs back so that the under-arches of each foot rest upon the curves of my firm buttocks. I know how my flexibility pleases her and I can feel her smile without even seeing her face. She lifts my hands so that they rest upon my ankles and binds feet and hands together in a package. I am ready.

Sometimes she suspends me, setting me against her wall for decoration, but not today. Today I will serve a more immediate purpose.

My face is turned the other way but I can hear the leather of the chaise longue sigh as she sits upon it. I hear her pour more wine into the glass. Moments later I feel the full glass laid to rest in my bound hands. Already the tight rope is producing pins and needles over my skin. I pray that my hands do not lose feeling altogether or else I shall drop the wine and displease her. I hear her rise again and walk over to the far corner of the room, the pointed heels of her boots clicking against the slate. She returns with a vase of blood-red roses. Parting my knees with the toe of her boot, she slides the vase between them.

'There,' she says. 'Now you look even more beautiful.'

I grip my knees together. I can feel the weight of the vase and the water inside. If I lose concentration, even for a second, it will fall. My muscles begin to ache with the strain of it.

She sits again and, this time, I feel her sharp heel press firmly against my temple. Thus we remain for twenty minutes or so. The exercise is merely to test me, my obedience as a slave and my endurance. My only wish is to impress her. I know she is watching me, admiring her handiwork and the way the ropes encase my body and package it so neatly. Every muscle in my body burns. I press my fingers against the glass to retain feeling in them.

Eventually she takes the vase from my knees and the glass from my hands. I slump, allowing my body to finally relax. I feel as though I've run a marathon. Her hands move over me, untying the ropes. I glance down and see the indentations they've made on my skin. How beautiful they look!

She lays me down flat while the blood rushes back into my veins. When she is satisfied I'm recovered, she addresses me again.

'Kneel.'

I obey. I wonder if I have pleased or disappointed her. Will I be rewarded or disciplined? Will she grant me pleasure or pain? She smiles, enjoying the anticipation on my face. She walks over towards the ivory chest. I strain my eyes to see what she will fetch, but to my surprise she walks straight past it to the open doorway.

I wait patiently.

My mouth drops open in amazement when she returns, for she leads behind her a tall girl, perhaps three years older than me. Like me, she wears nothing except a thick metal collar. Her skin is the colour of milk and her large breasts sway with the motion of her step. Her hair is white-blonde and reaches to below her hips. She is made to kneel beside me. My goddess leans over us. Her eyes are dancing.

'I have a treat for you, little one. I bring you a companion. This is Swan. She belongs to a colleague of mine who has kindly let me borrow her for the day. It will amuse me to watch the two of you together. She has been a slave for far longer than you. I thought you might benefit from her experience.'

It is true. I could see how well trained she is from the very first moment I saw her. Her eyes remain downcast the whole time. She has not even stolen a glimpse at me nor will she until she is instructed to do so. I feel clumsy and foolish next to her. A thread of envy begins to scrape my insides but I push it away and stare dutifully at the floor. I vow silently to myself that I will be as perfect a slave as she one day.

'Firstly, I wish to see the two of you wrestle,' says Mistress. 'Go!'

My heart misses a beat. Swan is about a foot taller than I am and stocky with it. My reflexes are quicker than hers. I see her lunge towards me and twist out of her way just in time. I catch hold of her hair and pull. She winces and yanks it out of my fingers. We circle each other, pacing one way then the other. Her mane of blonde hair makes her seem like a lioness about to pounce on its prey. She makes another sweep at me and this time seizes my wrist. She bends it at the elbow and forces it into my back. Her body presses against me, gripping tightly. I wriggle to free myself but her other hand clamps over my mouth, steadying her hold. With my free hand I reach back and pinch the sensitive skin between her thighs. She lets go immediately, and seeing my chance I leap on top of her. My hands grab her breasts and squeeze. She screams and shakes me off. I land with a thud against the hard floor, grazing my knee. In a trice she has pinned me down, pressing her fleshy buttocks into my back. I pound the floor with my fists and kick my legs furiously but her weight holds me securely. I have no choice but to concede defeat.

'Well done, Swan,' Mistress applauds. 'I give her to you as a reward. Play with her as you wish.'

Swan climbs off my back and kneels beside me. I remain flat on my stomach, uncertain as to what she will choose to do with me. She gazes down at me. The lioness becomes as gentle as a lamb. She strokes me with the fascination of a small child with a new doll. Her long, elegant fingers slip down from the crown of my head, combing through my chestnut tresses, sliding over the smooth skin at the base of my arched spine. Then the hands spread outwards, round my hips and cup my silken buttocks with the firmness of total devotion. I feel her delicate hands wash over my receptive bottom, tracing spiralling circles on each velveteen buttock and then dipping curiously to probe the secret place between them.

'She is beautiful, isn't she?' Mistress croons teasingly. Swan nods her agreement. 'Would you like to punish her? Would you like to chastise her lovely ass? Would you like to hear the cute little noises she makes when she is spanked?'

'Yes, Mistress,' she answers without hesitation.

My clitoris stirs and I sense the warm beginnings of a liquid response. I long for Swan's greedy palms to bite into my succulent flesh. Again Mistress's smooth, deep voice bathes our ears. It has the texture of warm chocolate as she addresses me.

'Little one,' she whispers. 'Do you want Swan to spank you?'

'Yes, yes, Mistress,' I whisper hoarsely, choked with emotion. 'Please let her punish me.'

'Well, Swan,' Mistress grins, turning to the athletic girl, 'my little slave has the most beautiful bottom in the world. Such beauty must not go unpunished and it *shall* not. Let her ass bewitch you. Let it cast a spell over your hands and attract them to it like a magnet. Allow your hands to pay it homage with punishment.'

In the large mirror in the corner of the room I can see her charming image as she straddles me backwards, a terrible queen about to execute her will over her humble subject. She leans forward over my accessible bottom and her impossibly long hair brushes against my sensitive skin. It feels like begin draped in a silk scarf. I wriggle. She notices my ticklishness.

Her fingers trickle over my naked curves, titillating me beyond control. She caresses the peachy flesh, warming it up in preparation for the smacks. I fear I will cum before the first spank has landed. I force the orgasm back. I want to prolong this feeling. She whispers to me so softly I do not think Mistress hears her.

'Such a privilege to polish a jewel as fine as this!'

I feel the first kiss of her palm. The acute sound echoes around the room and the feeling is delicious. My eyes close in ecstasy and my cunt begins to throb. She begins to spank me, her hands falling sharply on my rounded orbs. I can feel them growing pink. I know how lovely they look when they're that colour. I am certain that Swan is as aroused as I. I can feel the wetness of her pussy against my spine. She begins to push it into me, sliding it up and down against my skin. The more excited she becomes, the harder she spanks me. My skin is electrified. Her other hand joins in and she pummels my buttocks like a drum. I squeak. I squeal. I yelp like a puppy. My whimpers only seem to invite more kisses from her palms. My cunt drips, the moisture glistening from the deep crevice between my cheeks. Her grinding increases when she sees it. Her own pussy erupts and I feel her wet heat spill onto me. Her body collapses onto mine. Her hard nipples squash into my buttocks. Her heart pounds and I can feel every one of her body's shudders.

'Bravo!' Mistress cries. 'An excellent show, my darlings. I hope you have saved some of your sweet nectar for me. I have only just begun to enjoy myself.'

She rises and walks over to her ivory chest once more. From its depths she produces a large leather belt onto which is moulded a black rubber phallus in the very position a man's erect penis would be.

'Now, which of my slaves shall I make into a boy?' she ponders playfully. 'Swan, you've had your fun spanking my little one. I think I shall make her use this on you.'

Swan pauses for a moment, eyeing the huge ebony dildo attached to the belt in Mistress's hand.

'Yes, Mistress,' she murmurs.

Mistress nods for me to stand and I obey nervously. I have never worn anything like this and hope I will be competent, that I will not disappoint her or Swan. She secures the dildo in place. I am delighted to discover it has a small knob of soft rubber inside the belt that fits over my clit. Mistress buckles it tightly to my waist.

I glance at myself in the mirror. It looks so strange – a huge penis protruding from my groin! It makes me feel powerful. It seems to endow me with male lust. I cannot wait to shove it inside Swan's juicy pussy, to fuck her in return for spanking me. To fuck her as a man would.

Swan kneels on all fours, offering herself to me. The fleshy, rounded globes part to reveal her target, already saturated by her first orgasm. She wiggles her bottom invitingly. I kneel behind her, mounting her in the way the bull mounts the heifer. I grip the huge dildo with my hand to guide it. I aim it over her gaping hole and then push forward. I feel a slight tension as it squeezes against the inner walls of her pussy. I am surprised how easily it slides into her. She does not show me the slightest resistance, a true slave in all respects.

I move my pelvis back to draw it outwards again. I begin slowly but, as my confidence grows and I quickly learn the correct angle and motion, I begin to pump her with a steady rhythm. A long sigh escapes her. Perhaps she is letting me know I am not hurting her, that she is enjoying what I am doing to her.

Mistress walks back to her couch and reclines there with her wine, eyes glued to the scene before her.

I begin to really work the implement. My other hand slides down to rest on Swan's clit. The mound of flesh has grown enormous with her excitement. Each time I thrust the knob of rubber presses against my own and the friction is divine. I begin to circle my fingers around her flesh. She moans as I do so. I can feel her second orgasm building, greater than the first. I quicken my pace, fucking her with devoted vigour. She pushes back against the dildo, forcing it deeper inside. I can hardly believe the change in her. The formerly placid girl lets her moans grow more intense. Her head tosses back and forth, sending her mass of hair flying. Leaning forward over her, I whisper in her ear.

'It's such an honour to fuck a cunt as divine as this.'

The dirtiness of my words incites her explosion. Her cream seeps down the sides of the black rubber, drenching it, making it shine. She falls to the floor and her whole body thrashes about wildly. I catch her in my arms and press my lips to hers. My wet tongue traces the inside of her mouth and hers swirls around mine. I cuddle her tightly until she is calm once more.

'Thank you,' she smiles.

'Why should I let my slaves have all the fun?' Mistress cries suddenly, and I know her wish without having to wait for a command. She slides back on her couch and parts her muscular legs, unclipping the crotch of her basque to allow me access to her pussy. Swan helps to release me from the strap-on cock and I stand before my Mistress's ravenous pussy. She looks so majestic sitting there, legs akimbo and cunt thrust forward demanding my attention. I assume the position she prefers me in, bending at the waist with straight back and legs, balancing on tiptoe. She likes a good view of my ass in the mirror as I administer to her.

My skilful tongue goes to work on her. I know she likes nothing better than this type of pleasure. The perfection of such an art was one of my first lessons as her slave. I know my Mistress's body better than any adoring husband could. My tongue darts across her skin, tracing a line from her anus to her budding clit. I let my saliva cover it, making it glisten. Her hand rests firmly on my head. Swan has been watching the scene inquisitively. Mistress looks in her direction.

'Swan, my darling, I think your beautiful long hair would make an excellent whip for my little one's pussy.'

Twisting her long hair together, Swan walks over to stand directly behind me. I feel Mistress's boot against my knee, forcing my legs wider apart so that my sex pouts.

My rosebud grows to twice its size at the first stroke. The silky hair whips round between by legs, the ends flicking against my button. I have often felt Mistress's whips in this area but the texture of the fine hair is nothing like I have felt before. It stings sharply, yet its caresses are soft and delicate. It is like being kissed and bitten at the same time. Swan begins to whip me enthusiastically, alternating between my rosy buttocks and my sex. From time to time she pauses, allowing the waterfall of hair to slide between my buttocks and tickle my anus. She moves it up and down, letting it glide over my tight little hole. Then the whipping begins again, setting my pussy and my ass afire. The ends of the hair are like hundreds of little needles against my tender skin. My face remains glued to Mistress's cunt. I probe my tongue inside her with every stroke I receive. I am filled with the glorious smell and taste of her sex. I am ready to burst. She must see it in my eyes because she holds up her finger in warning.

'No, little one,' she teases. 'I do not permit you to cum yet. First you must bring me to orgasm. Only then may you give me yours.'

She is right. Her pleasure must come first. I, again, delay my own orgasm. Mistress, in a fit of wickedness, leans forward to swirl her expert fingers around my erect nipples, trying to tease my juices from me. Still I hold back. I can tell she is impressed with me. She leans back and lets the wave of orgasm flood her body. Her liquids wash onto my tongue. I suck and swallow every last drop of her sweet cum like I am trained to. I am joyous to be granted such a privilege, to drink of my goddess. I cannot hold back any longer. I know I am about to explode at any moment. Finally, Mistress nods to me.

'Very well, little one. Cum for me. Do it!'

Never have I been so eager to obey. My eyes close and my brow creases with the weight of the orgasm. Cum seeps from my pussy, covering the ends of Swan's hair. She continues to whip me as I orgasm, flogging the fresh honey from my sex. My eyelids close and I collapse on the floor in a cloud of uninhibited bliss. I faint, overwhelmed with more pleasure than my little body can take.

When I open my eyes again, I am greeted by my goddess's beaming face. Swan is nowhere to be seen. I presume that, her purpose served, she has been returned to her Mistress. I am disappointed that she is gone but glad to be alone again with my goddess. Still groggy, I drag myself into a kneeling position.

'I am proud of you, little one,' she smiles. 'You did very well today. I think that Swan was a good influence on you. Tell me, did you enjoy my treat?'

'Oh yes, Mistress,' I breathe. She smiles, showing her row of small, perfect teeth.

'I am glad. I may arrange that she visit us again, though soon you will no longer need her. Every day you improve in your obedience. It will not be long before you surpass even her.'

Her fingertip descends to catch my chin and gently raises my face to meet with hers. For a moment I am completely happy. My unworthiness drops away from me like the skin of a snake and I fly with her. Such cruelty in her eyes but oh, such love, and I am cast twixt the extremes. She leads me again to my corner and bids me sleep. She blesses my forehead with a kiss. I watch as she walks over to blow out the candle and closes the door behind her. The darkness surrounds me. It wraps me in its thick cloak of black. The hazy world of dreams overtakes me. I sleep, cradled in the grateful knowledge that I have pleased my goddess.

# Lolita

*I started my modelling career in teen fashion (before I was legally allowed to pose for bondage pictures). My little-girl looks quickly gained me the nickname of Lolita. The Nabokov novel has a notorious reputation (mainly to people who have never read it) because of its misconceived associations with paedophilia. If one actually takes the time to read it, one finds that its theme dwells more upon forbidden obsession and the story is told with tremendous beauty. I love the element of tease in my work, to show you what you desire but cannot have. In this poem, I am speaking both as a model and as a girl who enjoys being admired.*

*A mirage of fruit forbidden*
*Allowed to flicker once,*
*And only once,*
*In the box where your darkest fantasies stir*
*The seed sprouts*
*Begins to breathe*
*Stems reach out towards you*
*They want you*
*Need you*
*Blossoms awaken and begin to sparkle*
*Crimson rosebuds delight your eye*
*Tease you*
*Stoke your fire*
*Their scent sweet as poison*

*And vision,*
*Desire in its purest.*
*Come closer*
*Lead her to that place*
*Gaze, smell, listen, touch, taste*
*But beware the thorns.*

\*\*\*

# Redemption

*This is a tale of a darker nature. My fantasies exist on many different levels and, whilst I am often satisfied with more light-hearted escapades, occasionally I crave a more serious and sinister punishment. I dream of being controlled, humiliated and abused, like De Sade's Justine, an innocent and helpless pawn to the whims of those in power. It is a dangerous fantasy, best left to the imagination, but this book would not be complete without it. The cruelty, hypocrisy and injustice of the witch trials seemed an appropriate backdrop for the story.*

She had been fortunate. If her own dear father had not governed the town she would be suffering a fate far worse, following the ancient crones with the humped backs and wart-ridden faces to a fiery death amidst the purifying ashes.

She knew she should have been grateful to escape this fate, but as the muscular arms of the guard pulled her along the street, she almost wished for it. She gazed at the mocking faces of the townsfolk. Every good Christian soul had seen fit to attend – the schoolmasters who taught her the privilege of letters and numbers, the tailor who sewed together her dresses, the friends with whom she used to play. Most shook their heads in disgust and a grey-haired lady spat at her as she passed. She glanced through the sea of faces for her father's but he was nowhere to be seen. She was not surprised. His shame would not permit him to leave the house for a very long time. She hung her head, knowing she was the cause of that shame.

All she had done was dance. What harm was there in dancing? The moon had been full that night and lit her path through the forest as though with a purpose. A wolf let forth its mournful lament but the girl was not afraid. She had never feared these stormy-coated colleagues that shared the darkness with her. She opened her throat and joined in with the mournful chorus. The sound threaded its way around her heart and poured out through the circle of her mouth.

It did not take her long to find the circle of rocks. So the tales were true. Witches really did come up here. She stood in the very centre of the circle. Suddenly everything seemed clear to her. Her hands reached up and unthreaded the lace of her blouse. She let it drop to the ground. She looked down and saw the moonlight on her bare arms, bathing them with blue embers. A breeze shook the trees but she was not cold. She loosened her skirt and allowed it to join her blouse on the ground.

It was curiosity. Nothing more. She slowly raised her hands above her head and began to sway her hips as she had seen the gypsy women do when she was a little girl, before they were driven from the town. The dance began slowly. She was rather unsure of herself. All she knew was that she felt free without her clothes, a part of nature and in being such, more powerful than God himself.

Her movements grew wilder in her joy. She leapt high into the air and fell back to the earth on all fours like a beast. She felt the glory of the dirt beneath her palms and her knees. She moved her hips in wide circles. She arched her back like a cat and shook her mane of dark hair from side to side, letting it fall around her shoulders like a river. All of a sudden she realised she was no longer staring at the ground beneath her but at her own body far below. She could see the circle of stones and the wild figure spinning in the centre of them. She marvelled how beautiful the figure looked, its endless curves gyrating in the moonlight. Was that really she?

A twig snapped nearby and she felt herself hurtle back down to the earth to become one with her body again. She spun round to catch a glimpse of the pair of eyes glistening in the darkness. Her heart leapt. Perhaps her dancing really had summoned the devil himself. But as she peered into the darkness she could make out the auburn-haired form of Thomas Cuttle, partly hidden by one of the trees. She did not know how long he'd been there. Surely long enough to see what she'd been doing.

'Thomas!' she called. 'Promise me you won't tell!'

She could see his teeth gleam in the light. His face, covered with the freckles that she and the others had teased him about so often at school, broke into a grin; the smile of one who has finally been granted power. He started to move towards the town. She called after him, desperately grabbing her clothes from the ground.

'Thomas, stop! I'm warning you!'

Her brain searched for words in panic.

'If you tell then I'll... I'll get Lucifer to put a curse on you!'

The boy did not stop. She ran as fast as she could but by the time she'd thrown on her clothes he was way ahead of her. The bushes tore at her skirt as she ran back and tears blurred in her eyes. Twice she stumbled, the brown of the earth staining her blouse. Each time she picked herself up and continued running. She did not stop until she reached her father's house.

She could hear voices within. Grave voices speaking in low murmurs. Her first instinct was to run away. But where could she go? She pushed the door timidly and entered the room. Three faces turned to stare at her, their features distorted to seem even fiercer by the flickering candlelight. Thomas wore an expression of determination she had never seen in him before. His father stood next to him, shaking his head at the wretched girl. The other pair of eyes she dared not meet. They belonged to her father. He looked as though he'd aged ten years since this morning. His whole body trembled.

'We will leave her to your preparation,' said Mr Cuttle. 'The trial will be tomorrow. In the public court.'

'I beg you, Cuttle, could she not be tried in private?'

'I am afraid that is impossible. It is the will of the Lord that she is made an example of. People must learn that anyone, even the daughter of their beloved governor, can fall from grace into the hands of Satan.'

The girl could no longer hold her peace.

'I have done no such thing! I was only walking in the woods. There is no crime in that!'

'Walking? And I suppose you got so warm 'walking' that you felt the need to shed your garments?'

'That is not true!' She glared at Thomas. 'He has been waiting for a chance to punish me. Look at him, father! His ugliness must be the work of Lucifer. It is he who should be on trial, not me!'

A choked laugh escaped Mr Cuttle's cracked lips.

'Are you suggesting that my boy is a liar? Do you really think that the rest of the town will take the word of a foolish girl over his? We have eyes, my dear. Do you think we are blind to the way you lift the hem of your skirt whenever you walk past the boys in the square? Everyone has witnessed the devil beginning to exert his will over you. It was only a matter of time until you proved what you are.'

Her tears flowed over her stained clothes. Cuttle turned back to her father.

'We will bid you a good evening. I suggest you prepare your daughter for tomorrow. Of course, you will wish to beat her but please make certain she is at the courthouse by noon. May God have mercy on her soul.'

Neither the boy nor his father glanced at her as they left. Her father turned his back to her and she knew he was fighting back tears, too ashamed to even look at her. A part of her craved his temper, the stroke of his cane. This would be the first step of her penance for the shame she had brought to the family, but no such relief was granted. He said nothing.

'Father,' she said, her voice croaking through her sobs. 'I am sorry. So, so sorry.'

He did not answer, but pointed towards the stairs.

'Please, speak to me...'

She knew it was useless. She staggered up the stairs to her room and lay on her bed, her sobs piercing the dark silence. She prayed with all her soul. She knew the penalty for witchcraft and she would surely be found guilty. The only tools of hope were her youth and her father's status in the town.

After about an hour she heard her father's footsteps climbing the stairs. For a blessed moment she thought he would deliver the absolution with the rod that she so desperately needed, but the expectation was short-lived. The footsteps continued past her door and disappeared into the room of her father. He meant to leave her alone with her guilt.

She could barely remember the trial. Fear had seized her and distorted her memory. Vague images floated in her mind of saturated garments clinging tightly to her skin; the icy chill of the river's currents; her chest clenching like a fist in agony as it fought for air; the panic as she had struggled to set herself free and swim to the surface. She must have screamed out her guilt, else she would have shared the watery fate of the innocents before her.

She recalled the angry shouts of protest when her fate was announced – the furious cries that she did not deserve such leniency. There were those who had called for more traditional methods of punishing the crime of conspiring with the evil one, but her father's word was law and he would not allow them. The decision would cost him his position but save his only daughter's life. Furious as he was, he could not bear to see her put to death, even if she was a child of Satan. His pleas had been passionate. He had sworn it was the foolishness of youth that consumed his daughter and begged that she be cleansed of her sins and given a second chance. It may have been the roused words of the father or the prettiness of the girl that melted the hearts of the court, but eventually the townsfolk succumbed to his view and agreed that she would pay for the sins of her soul with her flesh.

The arm of the pillory was raised as she neared it. The guard pushed her forward onto the platform in the centre of the square and made her bend over the waiting restraint. Two men in faun leather hoods grabbed her hands and thrust them into the semicircular grooves in the oak. A third forced down her head and the wood scraped against her soft neck. She was held in there as the wood sealed her in place and the heavy locks were secured on either side, preventing any chance of escape.

She kept her eyes down, not daring to meet those of the good folk gathering around the scene. Their taunting shouts were like daggers in her ears, and with her arms locked beneath the heavy oak she could do nothing to shut them out.

She gasped as something brushed her cheek and smashed into the wood by her head. The stench told her that it had been a goose's egg, long rotten. She heard a mother scold a child for its impatience.

The din of the crowd died and she knew that her punisher must have mounted the platform. She could feel his presence moving behind her. He circled round and came to stand in front of the pillory. She could see the black shoes on the platform before her. She could make out her own terrified face in the shine of the buckles, and her horror grew as she recognised Cuttle's voice.

'You have admitted your guilt in making a pact with Satan and committing a shameless act of immorality. It has been decided that due to the tenderness of your age and the weakness of your sex, you could not have been in possession of your own senses. It is the Lord's holy will that the influence of the evil one be struck out of you with the rod so that your soul may join Him once more.'

The crowd grunted its approval. Cuttle leant down to her, pressing his lips so close to her ear that she could feel his hot, fetid breath. She heard his coarse, cruel whisper.

'And I can assure you that your purification will be most thorough.'

Hatred bubbled up through her veins. For a split second she willed him to burn in the brimstone of hell. Turning her head towards him she spat with all her strength into his bulbous face. The townsfolk hushed. Cuttle straightened and put his hand to his cheek. Suddenly, he broke the silence with a roar of laugher.

'Behold,' he cried to the onlookers. 'See how even now the hell-cat mocks the righteous!'

The crowd joined his guffawing. She glanced down and saw the feet disappear from her periphery and until she could only hear the click of the heels on the wooden platform. The two figures that had helped to secure her appeared on either side. Each grabbed the hem of her skirts and lifted them to the height of her shoulder blades and pinned them in place. She felt the breeze caress her naked back and buttocks, now helplessly exposed to the wrath and vengeance of God. Her shame engulfed her. It was one thing to shed her clothing in the forest at night when she was certain she was alone, but quite another to be deliberately stripped of covering before the attentive eyes of all she knew. She had sinned. There was no denying that and she did wish to atone for her misdeeds, but she was prisoner to her own cowardice.

The voice behind her announced the words she was dreading.

'In the name of the Lord, may this child of sin repent!'

No sooner had the final syllable been uttered than the switch fell, cutting the curved orbs of her buttocks in two. There was a moment of numbness and then the pain reached her senses. She gritted her teeth, determined not to give her punisher the satisfaction of her cries.

The rod cut again, a more carefully directed blow stinging the tender region at the tops of her thighs. This time she could not hold back the tears. A hearty welt was already beginning to emerge on the flawless skin. Cuttle noticed this and attacked again in the same spot with his full strength. It would show that he was doing his job efficiently. The girl let out a guttural scream and the crowd erupted in a cheer. Cuttle smiled, the noise reinforcing his position of power. He began to lay into his penitent, the strikes coming thick and fast. She squirmed and pulled back, trying to get her head and arms free. Her efforts were useless and only incited more mirth from the crowd. Scarlet rivets marking the paces where the switch had kissed flesh sprung up all over her. Her bottom was swollen and raw. Many of the male townsfolk pushed round to the back of the platform to obtain a better view of the bruised target, calling to their wives that Cuttle was indeed showing conscientiousness with the chastisement of the witch.

'Confess!' Cuttle yelled as his arm descended again towards her exposed and sorry posterior. 'Let the world hear your remorse.'

Her pride had shrivelled long before and the words spilled out through her sobs.

'I am sorry. Dear Lord, forgive me. I have sinned against you and I am sorry. I repent. I repent.'

The good folk cheered their approval. As she spoke the words she felt a weight lift from her soul. Each strike chipped away part of her guilt. The pain purified her. Her trespasses dissolved with her tears on the platform by her feet.

One final blow from the switch and the townsfolk were let loose upon her to complete her penance. They swarmed around the platform on all sides, hurling all they could spare, showering her in a putrid pulp of decayed tomatoes, cabbage, onions and eggs. The mess lodged in her hair and covered every inch of her skin. The acid of the tomatoes seeped into her welts and stung her. The crowd roared at the sight, the haughty governor's daughter sorrowful and drenched in muck.

Eventually the crowd dispersed and went about their business, invigorated by the morning's entertainment. Some ignored her. Some laughed and pointed as they passed. Some of the men spent a little longer than usual ogling her displayed breasts or the sight of her naked curves glistening with the slime of the rotten vegetables.

She would remain there until the following day as a reminder to other witches. Although her entire body stung and it would be a long time before she regained the popularity she had enjoyed within the town, her relief was heartfelt. She had shown penitence and would be granted redemption.

There was no moon that night. It had hidden itself behind the clouds as though she did not deserve the privilege of its light. She shivered with cold and every noise made her jump. The putrid food about her feet provided a hearty feast for the town's healthy population of rats. Once or twice one scuttled across her bare toes and she screamed so loud that some of the townsfolk appeared in their windows and cursed her for disturbing their rest.

The rats had eaten until their stomachs were bursting and then left her in peace, and she was just beginning to enter the doze of exhaustion when a clammy hand was clamped over her mouth. It remained there until her muffled squeals and struggles subsided and was then replaced by a wet, knotted rag tied firmly at the back of her head. The material served its purpose. It had been drenched in spirits helping to dull both the sound of her cries and the sharpness of her senses. Even if she had not recognised his voice, she would have known her attacker from his odour.

'What good fortune! Here is a pretty little sinner. I must thank you, my girl. The town is certain to elect me to be their new governor now that they've seen your father cannot even retain control of his own child. Well, Thomas, you told me you desired her. Do you still find her so fair now that her form is covered in the welts of her trespasses and her face is stained with the tears of repentance?'

Her eyes widened. Had he really brought his wretched son to share his depravity? Yes, she instantly recognised the snide voice of her schoolmate.

'You speak the truth, father. She has no right to think herself more worthy than I now.'

'Then watch with a keen eye, my son, and I will teach thee the proper treatment for a girl of sin.'

She tried again to scream as she felt the rough hands scoop around her waist and cup lustily the curves of her breasts. He squeezed her nipples ferociously between his clumsy fingertips. His waist pressed tight against the bare curves of her buttocks. Renewed fire burst in the welts left by the switch, but her whimpering seemed to fan his lust.

'It seems only fitting that I take her in the devil's hole. The resistance of the flesh there is so much sweeter.'

The hands left her breasts and reached down around her buttocks. Gripping the flesh firmly he parted the orbs and she felt a pain far worse than any blow from the rod. It shot through her and she almost lost consciousness. Cuttle pushed against her, emitting grunts like those of a swine. Her neck and wrists were forced forward as her body was jolted against the pillory. Fresh tears stained her cheeks. The man's sweaty mass shunted against her, devouring such young and beautiful flesh as he had not tasted since his wife was in her prime. The girl's body fought him but there was no escape. She could only imagine that this was the final stage of God's punishment. Perhaps she had to be reduced to nothing, to a mere whore, before she would be worthy to be accepted into heaven.

Nearby, Thomas watched the scene with interest. Cuttle glanced in his direction and barked at his useless offspring.

'What are you waiting for, you damned fool? Force her mouth open. Make her swallow you!'

Thomas jumped at his father's orders and slunk over to her. She smelt the spirits on his breath. He lowered his breeches. She shut her eyes tightly. The boy slapped her face, instantly bruising her jaw.

'You are going to pay for the way you torment me. You are going to learn the penalty for being a temptress, for sending out your spirit to haunt my dreams every night and make me cover the bed with Satan's liquid.'

He ripped the material from her mouth and thrust the head of his manhood down her throat. She almost gagged under the full flesh. She tried to bite but could not close her mouth. He shoved against her awkwardly, forcing her to take his manhood, knowing she was powerless to stop him.

The boy had eaten his fill in no time, shooting the milky liquid deep into her throat before pulling his flesh hurriedly back into his breeches. The father continued to shove against her, his thrusts growing more and more vigorous. His sex felt as though it grew more swollen every time it drove into her. His panting grew louder and she began to pray to God or to anyone who would listen, knowing he was about to fill her from the other side.

But then she heard a sudden dull thud behind her and Cuttle's form slumped to the platform. She peered into the darkness but the pillory prevented her view. A scuffling followed and Thomas joined his father in the dirt. The man and boy groaned.

'Rest assured that the good people of the town will hear of this.'

She recognised the deep voice of her father. Cuttle struggled to his feet, dragging the startled boy up with him.

'Let them hear! What will they care if I use a witch as the whore she is?'

'But she is no longer the devil's companion,' said her father calmly. 'The whole town witnessed her repentance and the Lord's forgiveness. You have assaulted an innocent!'

Cuttle froze. It was true. No one could deny they saw the girl pay the price of her sins and return to God's grace. Attacking an innocent was a crime punishable by death. Her father pulled the shaken man's coat in his fists so that Cuttle's face was only an inch away from his. She had never heard such ferocity in her father's voice.

'Leave... *now!*'

The next day a party were sent to search for the man and his son, but they were never seen in the town again. She was careful in future never to do anything to allow her father's pride in her diminish, even for a second. She and her father were quick to regain respect in the town. She was commended for taking her punishment so well and for her saintly endurance of the fiends that night. Several young men who had observed the purification offered proposals of marriage but she refused, saying she was not yet ready.

She still ventured into the forest but stayed well clear of the circle of rocks, and she was always careful to return to the village before nightfall.

# Libertinage

*This was one of the first erotic stories I ever wrote. At the time of writing, my mind was more full of lust than literature and for that reason, the tone of this piece is more primal and raw than many others in this book. The plot is loosely inspired by* La Philosophie dans le Boudoir *by the Marquis de Sade. I chanced upon this work three short years ago, when I had just turned sixteen. I found that I truly related to the character of Eugenie. I yearned to be 'educated' into the ways of the flesh as she was, and wondered if I would prove as eager and as excellent a pupil. I wanted to tell the story from her perspective and felt that the decadent lifestyle of modern day uptown New York would provide the perfect setting.*

This had to be the place. 154 Westward Avenue. That was the address neatly penned into the front of my diary. I pushed through the revolving doors, my fingers leaving their prints upon the glass. The security guard raised his head from behind the pages of a coffee-stained newspaper.

'Can I help you, miss?'

I smirked. The thick Noo Yawk accent would take some getting used to, but I didn't mind. It reminded me that I was on holiday and a long way from home.

'Yes, thank you. I'm looking for apartment number 207.'

'Where you from? Australia?'

'England, actually.'

'You here all alone? You oughta be careful. Pretty thing like you.'

'I'm meeting a friend of my father.'

'I see. That's good. What apartment did you say again?'

'207.'

'Twentieth floor and turn right. Elevator's over there.'

I thanked him and hurried across the lobby in the direction he had shown. I could feel his eyes watching me as I went and heard him mutter when he thought I was out of earshot. 'Unless you'd like to get your pretty lips around this.'

I ignored it and pressed the button for the twentieth floor. I couldn't help feeling anxious. It was silly but I felt like I was on a journey into the unknown. It was my first trip alone to America, or anywhere else, for that matter. I had always been a bit shy and I hadn't seen Lady Crystal since she paid us a visit in London the previous summer. Lady Crystal was Lady by budget rather than birth. She had purchased the title for a lark during one of her trips to 'Old Blighty', but somehow it suited her. She always carried herself with such aristocratic sophistication and confidence. Even my father had taken to calling her the Lady.

The elevator doors parted and I walked down the long hallway, scanning the doors for the numbers. I reached 207 at last and waited for a moment, sleeking my hair down and straightening my top. The moment I tapped the brass knocker the door was flung open and I was caught up in the tanned arms of Lady Crystal and twirled around the room.

'My sweet angel! It's so wonderful to see you again. Let me look at you. Well now! My little English rose has bloomed! You were a schoolgirl in braids and spectacles when last I saw you and now look at you!'

She looked even more amazing than I had remembered her. Her white-blonde hair fell about her shoulders in sculptured waves. I had almost died when she told me how much she paid her private stylist but I figured that to look so stunning the price was worth it. Her hazel eyes shone at me from beneath impossibly long lashes.

I couldn't keep my eyes off her when she'd visited us. She was the most perfect looking woman I had ever seen. She had noticed me staring and smiled back, but I instantly blushed and pretended to be studying something on the floor. Now I could feel my face becoming flushed again, simply being in her presence.

She embraced me in that delightful way that she'd done when she visited my family in London the year before, letting her fingers trickle lightly down my spine and come to rest where the material of my jeans sunk into the deep taut cleft between my buttocks. It always made me tremble when she did this, though I wasn't sure why. I started to giggle.

'I missed you, Lady Crystal,' I said.

She took me into the living room where a monstrous breakfast had been prepared. I had eaten nothing but aeroplane dinners for a whole day and so dug heartily into the pile of pancakes with syrup, hash browns, scrambled eggs and fresh orange juice.

As I ate we caught up on the activities of the past year, and eventually the subject turned to boyfriends.

'What?' the Lady exclaimed. 'Eighteen years old and never had a boyfriend? My goodness, are they hiding you under a rock?'

'As good as,' I replied. 'Father thinks I'm still too young to go on dates.'

'I shall have to speak with him. Treating you like a child! Is he blind?'

'To tell you the truth, I'm a bit nervous,' I confessed. 'I really don't know anything so I'd probably just make a fool of myself even if I went on a date.'

'Well I'm glad you came to me, my girl. I promise you that by the time you return to England, you'll be able to take on any man you fancy.'

The stranger did not advance to greet me. He merely stood, legs apart and arms folded, ogling me with grey eyes. Though the rest of his face remained as stone, those eyes flickered with keen interest at my presence.

I had been with Lady Crystal for over a week now and was having the time of my life. She and I had just returned from Bloomingdales, where she treated me to a shopping spree. I knew she could more than afford it, but I was very grateful for her generosity. She even bought me some black lace knickers that would have caused my father to die had he seen them. I was delighted when the pristine woman in the lingerie department asked if I was a model!

I loved being with Lady Crystal and wished I could stay with her forever. Her life was so exciting, such a refreshing contrast to my dreary, over protected life at home. She gave me something I had never been given at home; she treated me like a woman instead of a naïve little girl. The more time I spent with her, the more my confidence grew. I wanted to be taken under her wing. I wanted to learn everything about her, everything about her wealthy and promiscuous lifestyle.

My head was light from an enormous lunch. Lady Crystal even bought me wine to wash it down.

'Your father doesn't let you drink either?' she had said.

'Right, your education begins now.'

I had downed three full glasses and was wrapped in a blissful contentment, giggling at almost everything my heroine said. I burst through the door of her apartment in a fit of laughter and almost jumped out of my skin when I saw the silver-haired, smooth-faced man dressed entirely in black seated in one of Lady Crystal's leather chairs.

'Don't worry, my darling,' the Lady teased, resting her hand on my shoulder. This is the Viscount. He is a dear friend and has agreed to assist me with a certain matter concerning your initiation into our little club'

She led me over to him. It was obvious that he shared the Lady's aristocratic flair and the confidence of money. His noble title, preposterous if given to anyone else, suited him.

He stood at last and took my face between his hands. He scrutinised me so thoroughly that my eyes widened and I actually gulped.

'Well, Viscount, what do you think?' the Lady asked. 'Isn't she all I promised?'

'Lovely,' he said at last. 'Truly lovely.'

'As you can see, Viscount, she's quite a step above most of the girls you have encountered in the past, in that her beauty is her own. Not a single cent has been spent to enhance that delicate, elfin bone structure, or that perfect, petite nose. She is as fresh and natural as the day she came out of the womb. Her lips possess such fullness, and hasn't she got the biggest, most doll-like emerald eyes you've ever seen?' The tone of the Lady's voice changed ever so slightly. 'I'll let you into a little secret. I've had the pleasure of glimpsing this little mademoiselle while she took a bath, and can assure you that her face is only the beginning of her charms.'

I blushed deeply at this, but Lady Crystal seemed perfectly at ease in her game, tantalising her guest with the spoken word. A sly smile formed upon the Viscount's lips. He spun me around so that my rear was towards him, and I was shocked to feel his hand upon the hem of my pleated skirt. But the Lady was quick to intervene, slapping the inquisitive hand playfully.

'Patience!' she scolded. 'You must wait a little longer for your prize. It will be all the more rewarding for it.'

'Very well,' he remarked. 'Her hidden beauty shall be revealed presently. You are more than aware of my tastes.' He fixed me with his gaze. 'Young lady, I trust your manners will match your external attractions. We are both counting on you to be a good pupil.' I nodded. 'You will listen with utmost attentiveness to the lessons we will give? You will learn quickly and make us proud of your progress?'

'Yes, sir,' I managed.

'Very well, Lady Crystal,' he announced, turning to her. 'I'm prepared to offer my services on one condition. You must leave her instruction entirely up to me. You must not interfere with or question my decisions.'

'As you wish, Viscount,' answered the Lady, with an ounce of humility I had never noticed in her before. The silver-haired man turned back to me.

'You have been taught nothing about the intimacies of men and women?'

I was not used to such a direct question and I could feel my face burn with embarrassment. At home, in a household still clinging to the principles of Victorian morality, we simply did not discuss such things. But I was determined to satisfy my curiosity and so I composed myself and summoned an answer.

'Nothing, sir.'

He smiled. 'Then we had better commence with your schooling right away.' He turned to the Lady. 'Would you be so kind as to draw the curtains and remove your blouse?'

I couldn't believe my ears and wondered for a second if I had heard correctly, but the elegant lady glided over to the window and shut out the view of the surrounding building and impatient bustle of noise from the streets far below. She lit one of the lamps, filling the room with a comfortable glow. It was as though we were in a cosy cave, as if the rest of the world no longer existed beyond the walls of the room.

The Lady obliged the second part of the Viscount's request without a moment's hesitation. I found her confidence inspiring, but at first I did not know where to rest my gaze. So often I had stared at her rounded breasts when I was certain she wasn't looking. How I loved and admired their shape! I liked the way she chose to wear tops so tight that the buttons of nipple protruded defiantly through the thin material, greeting the world. It did not take much for me to imagine what those lovely shapes looked like unhindered by their covering, but I never dreamed I would actually witness their nakedness for my own eyes, and so close.

They were magnificent! So full and round with large nipples erect so that they looked like fleshy dials. The humidity began to increase between my legs. It was not the first time it had happened. I'd noticed it before whenever the Lady's purposeful hand lingered on my rump for just a little longer than was socially acceptable, but this heat was more intense than before. At first I thought it was simply due to being confronted with the nakedness before me, but I gradually realised it was eagerness rather than embarrassment that engulfed me. I wanted to touch those beautiful symbols of womanhood, to feel their weight in my hands and nuzzle into the deep valley between them.

My face must have betrayed my desires, for Lady Crystal reached out and guided my eager hands to her. I shifted uncomfortably from one foot to the other as the slipperiness in my panties increased. I stroked the soft flesh, running my fingers over the smooth, pliant skin... but it wasn't enough. I needed more and that need gave me courage.

'Please,' I whispered, 'may I kiss them?'

'But of course you may, my darling,' she purred.

I did not need a second invitation. My mouth enclosed around the glorious nipples, moistening them, sucking them like a babe. I felt incredibly naughty to have such intimate objects resting under my tongue but the wickedness was delicious. Lady Crystal gasped in surprise and pleasure.

'The little minx!' she exclaimed. 'She's a natural.'

'Well, since she shows such an aptitude, perhaps I'll allow her to try her newly found skills on another worthy target,' announced the Viscount.

Lady Crystal looked at me.

'It's up to you, my angel,' she smiled. 'Do you feel ready for your initiation?'

Perhaps the wine helped to guide my actions, or perhaps it didn't, but in no time I found myself kneeling before him on the carpet, my blood pounding with excitement. Lady Crystal settled into a chair to watch the scene with keen interest. I undid the zip of his trousers, and reaching inside, I felt a bulge straining against his underpants. He took my wrist and guided my hand, helping me to take out their contents, and nothing could have prepared me for the sight before me. I had seen pictures of cocks before, giggling at the odd diagrams in my Anatomical Development class at school, but the real thing held such nobility! I studied its shape with a keen eye. I felt honoured to witness it, a proud and erect mark of power. I wrapped my hands fully around the shaft. For this I did not need coaching. The minute I felt the rigid muscle squeezed between my hands I just seemed to instinctively know what to do.

I started to work it with a slow, steady rhythm, glancing up at his face from time to time to see if I was performing to his satisfaction. I grew braver and allowed my mouth to close over the end, tasting its delicious juices. I felt his hand on my head, pushing me back.

'Stop,' he said calmly. 'Tell me what you are doing.'

I hesitated. I hadn't expected this. I marvelled that it was so humiliating to say the words when I was so willing to perform the action.

'I'm sucking your... your cock,' I mumbled, looking down at the carpet.

'What?' he asked. 'I didn't quite hear that. Say it again.'

'I'm sucking your cock,' I repeated.

'Again. Louder.'

'I'm sucking your *cock!*'

'That's better. Say it proudly. It is important that you understand the action, not just carry it out without any thought. Now get to work or I'll punish you.'

I returned to the task with haste. My pink tongue traced around the circumference of the flesh where the swollen head met the shaft. I licked vigorously from the base to the tip. I enclosed my lips around it, sucking it and sucking it, swirling it lovingly in the wetness of my mouth, making my lips travel deeper and deeper down the shaft. I felt it stiffen even harder and swell so large that I could barely fit it in my mouth. Then, taking me surprise and making me blink with shock, it erupted like a volcano, shooting its salty liquid onto my tongue and into my throat.

'That's it,' the Viscount breathed heavily. 'Now let's see you swallow every drop.'

I was only too happy to comply, letting his gorgeous cream slide down and warm my stomach. The Viscount seemed pleased.

'You show promise,' he said. 'I'm certain you will be quite a prodigy,' he remarked as he concealed his flesh behind the restraints of his trousers once more. 'Lady Crystal has done well to recommend you to me. Now I must rest for a minute and rekindle the fire of my passion. You have excelled at giving pleasure, so now I think you have earned the privilege of receiving it.'

I was thoroughly excited by the prospect. I could hardly wait. I stood, eager as a puppy, my ears crying out for my next instruction.

The Viscount slumped into a chair beside his companion and they both scrutinised me, their eyes gleaming at my enthusiasm. The Viscount leaned back.

'You seem to be wearing too many garments, hardly appropriate for the July heat. Remove your blouse for me.'

I had never been naked in front of a man before, and I felt my face growing crimson at the thought. At the same time I was beginning to find a surreptitious delight in misbehaving. I had kept my body respectably hidden beneath my clothes for long enough, and now I *wanted* to remove my blouse. I wanted to show them both how my body had blossomed. I wanted their eyes to feast on my nakedness.

I began undoing my puff-sleeved blouse, starting from the top button and then moving downwards towards my navel. I let it slip to the floor, leaving me standing in nothing but my skirt and bra, the white satin cupping my small, pert mounds with intimate care. I reached back and unhooked it.

My first concern was that my breasts might prove disappointing to my colleagues. I could not boast the ample chest of the Lady. But I should not have worried, for the Viscount's face lit up when he saw them.

'Why, they are as sweet as budding roses!' he exclaimed. 'And I bet they're as soft and velvety to the touch as the petals of that same flower.'

Lady Crystal nodded in agreement, and the two of them rose and advanced on me like ravenous wolves. They each took one dainty nipple in their mouth, tantalising it amorously. Heat shot through my body straight to the region between my thighs. My legs trembled and I felt my body sink as my knees began to give way. The Viscount lifted me over his broad shoulder and placed me in the large chair. My hands grasped at my breasts, the fingers pinching the sensitive nipples, trying to emulate the action of their mouths.

'She has quite an appetite, doesn't she?' said the Viscount. 'Such petite breasts are often bursting with sensitivity. But she is still hiding attributes that delight me even more. It's time the little tease is made to unveil them.'

Lady Crystal stretched out her hand to me and I took it. She lifted me from the chair and twirled me like a dancing partner until my bottom was presented to the Viscount. She pinched the hem of my skirt daintily in her fingertips and raised it until the base of my white cotton panties peeked out from beneath it, before letting it fall once more.

'You torture me, woman,' stated the Viscount, but Lady Crystal smiled broadly and undid the buttons at the back of my skirt. At last she whisked the skirt away from me in triumph, allowing the waiting gentleman a full view of my tightly sheathed bottom. She tossed the skirt to the sumptuous carpet, and shortly my panties met the same fate.

'Oh,' the Viscount crooned, 'I have never seen its equal. Such perfect curvature in the lines. Why, I do believe I spy a juicy peach simply begging for a bite.'

He sunk to his knees and buried his teeth into the object of his rapture. I squealed and giggled, and I could feel his tongue lapping the skin as a cat laps cream.

'Oh, divine,' he confirmed. 'So firm. Such silken elasticity in the skin. Let's see what pearl this fine oyster contains.'

His hands seized my buttocks, squeezing and kneading the taut flesh before prizing them gently apart to reveal the tiny pink star between. He pressed his nose deep into the cleft and then pressed my bum-cheeks around his face as though to smother himself.

'The scent is sweet,' he said. 'It begs for a taste.'

His hot tongue flickered, darting against the tight hole like a serpent's. Moisture burst from my femininity and ran down my thighs.

'Aha, what's this?' he remarked, surfacing to trace his finger through my silver slipperiness. 'Just look at this, Lady Crystal; the dirty little bitch enjoys the feel of my tongue upon her ass.'

At once his sodden fingers were in his mouth.

'Ecstasy!' he exclaimed. 'Her nectar is as fresh and sweet as honey straight from the hive. And now I must see the fountain from which this delicious elixir has sprung.'

He threw me on my back on the thick, maroon carpet and spread my lithe, athletic legs wide apart. The Lady knelt down to join him and the pair of them began to examine me as though they were doctors.

'What a delicate button,' the Lady gasped, 'and so big for such a petite girl! I'll wager it is even richer in sensitivity than her breasts.'

'You may enjoy her first,' said the Viscount, seating himself. 'I shall allow the sight to stir my pleasure.' He looked into my eyes.

'Now tell me, little angel, what would you like your beautiful Lady here to do with that heavenly little virgin cunt of yours?'

The word excited me. I had never heard anyone use it so openly before, and it sounded so deliciously dirty.

'Please,' I whispered, 'I want her to touch it, yes, I want her to lick it.'

'Then you had better beg her.'

I fought and conquered my embarrassment.

'Please, Lady Crystal. Please will you lick my cunt for me?'

'If you insist, my dear,' the Lady purred.

I felt her experienced fingers upon the lips of my swelling bulb, pulling them softly apart to show the baby-pink inside. Then it was her skilled tongue, tickling it with the tiniest tremble, teasing it rapidly from side to side. The rest of my body seemed to melt away and I was all cunt, thirsty for her touch. She began to lick at the opening to my vagina, pushing her tongue inside a little way, then a little further. Then her whole mouth enclosed my clitty. I felt the orgasm rise from deep inside. It was like a tidal wave passing over my entire body. The Lady drank up my hot cum as it poured from the mouth of my cunt. My lower regions tingled and still I wanted more.

The Viscount was only too willing to complete my lesson. He scooped me up in his arms and carried me, like a bride, into the Lady's bedchamber. Lady Crystal followed the procession and seated herself in a large armchair in the corner of the room. Tossing me down onto the silken sheets of the huge waterbed, he shed his clothing and joined me on his knees. The bed rocked under his weight. I leaned back and stretched out on my back, looking up at him expectantly. He looked at me for a long time, seeming to study every inch of my body, and came to rest finally on my compliant femininity.

'Little angel,' he breathed huskily. 'Your innocence makes you so delectable to corrupt. I have never tasted one as fine as you, and I admit I am tempted. But no, despite your pleading you are not yet ready. Let's leave your cunt untarnished... at least for the time being. It is a delicacy too beautiful to devour just yet. I shall take my pleasure in that other tight little place of which I'm so fond. If our angel will assume a position on her hands and knees, I will allow her a little sample of what she has been missing.'

Somewhat unsure of his intent, I obediently rolled over onto my stomach and lifted up on my hands and knees, and my innocent compliance seemed to inflame his cock even more.

'Yes,' he said to Lady Crystal. 'We'll make a seductress out of this virtuous girl yet.'

He took a moment to admire the view before him, and I couldn't help but egg him on, waggling my ass as I had seen lap dancers do on television. His lechery spilled into his limbs and he gripped my hips firmly and bent down over me.

'Now, my darling,' he whispered in my ear. 'This may hurt a little at first, but when the initial pinch subsides you will taste ecstasy like never before.'

Lady Crystal fetched a bottle of oil from her bedroom. The Viscount took it and poured its contents over my waiting buttocks and into the deep cleavage between. He smoothed it in with his finger, inserting the tip just inside my waiting anus. Then a little further until his whole finger was inside me. The feel of it was strange and a little painful, but true to the Viscount's promise, the sting soon transformed into quite a different sensation. He worked the oil thoroughly and coated his shaft with the other hand.

He withdrew his finger and I felt, almost immediately, the rigid tip of his cock squeezing into my bum. I winced and bit my lip as my flesh was prised open by his. He pushed inside, slowly at first and then building pace as my muscles began to relax to accommodate him. My body began to gyrate and I moaned softly. He was entering me with careful, steady thrusts, never breaking in rhythm but forcing himself deeper inside my channel.

Soon he was all the way in, my rounded buttocks bouncing against his muscular stomach as he rode me.

'My goodness, what a filthy little slut,' he grunted. 'Tell me what you are.'

'I'm a filthy little slut,' I moaned, and the pride in my words surprised everyone in the room, including me.

'That's right,' he grunted, 'and all filthy little sluts deserve to have their ass smacked.'

He continued to spear me with his cock, but his powerful hands began to slap my buttocks, spanking them heartily until they turned crimson and began to burn. I was amazed to find that the act aroused me further. It wasn't like the awful punishments I received from my father; my bottom stung delightfully and I started to see spankings in quite a different light. I wriggled my bottom against his cock.

'She's so naughty,' Lady Crystal said quietly, as though in awe. 'I insist you spank her harder.'

I squealed as the torrent of scorching spanks rapidly increased. I glanced over and saw The Lady watching us with legs akimbo, working her own dripping pussy with a large vibrator, her giant breasts swaying with the motion. I couldn't help myself. My fingers reached back to my clitty, massaging it as I was being fucked. Fucked! The very word turned me on.

'Do it!' I cried deliriously. 'Fuck my ass! Fuck me and lick me and suck me and spank me! I want it. I want it so badly!'

My orgasm rose again, far more intense than the first. The Viscount's cock felt like a rod of steel ramming my ass, and then with an almighty cry he gave one final plunge and sprayed his creamy cum deep into my hole, flooding it completely. Then as he pulled out my own orgasm was triggered and I collapsed, panting on my belly, my body convulsing with my pleasure. I had never dreamed that it was possible to feel like that.

'I trust our pupil has enjoyed her first little sample of forbidden fruit?' enquired the Lady, who lounged in a pool of her own moisture.

'Yes, thank you,' I panted. 'Thank you so much.'

'Well,' remarked the Viscount. 'I think we can all be proud. Our little angel has turned out to be quite the little devil in disguise. I congratulate you, dear girl. You are well on the way down the path of enlightenment. What a holiday we have in store for you, dear girl!'

My holiday in America was the most wonderful time of my life, but such times are often doomed to a short life. Part of me wanted to stay with Lady Crystal and the Viscount and continue to enjoy their life of excess, the American way, but the other part knew I must return home to England.

However, the girl who boarded the plane at JFK Airport was not the bashful innocent who had greeted New York for the first time a month before. I no longer dreaded returning home. My time in New York helped me realise that my sexuality had been stifled by me and not by my surroundings. I was eternally grateful to my dedicated tutors, but I could hardly wait to set foot on English soil again. I had been given the gift of wisdom and it was a gift I did not intend to waste.

*Freud's Vision*

# Arachne's Lair

*I wanted to write a bondage story with a difference. This piece of erotica was inspired by a spring morning in the garden. I lazed on the grass and watched a spider tightly binding an insect in shining thread. I wondered what it would be like to be ensnared in such a way. Surely there was never a cleverer or more sinister lady than she. Beautiful, skilful and deadly like a vampire, she would entice her innocent prey into her clutches, drug them with venom and keep them bound and helpless until she was ready to feast upon them.*

It is not thread alone that she weaves. She weaves a spell even more powerful, rendering my will as defenceless against her as my body. It was under the potency of that spell that I was brought here. Even now it intoxicates me, lightening my head in a blissful half-awakened haze. My back sealed tightly to my sticky prison, my body forms a cross with each limb pulled wide and every part of my front exposed. I can move my arms a little to the right or left if I use all my might, but I cannot prise them loose without her help. But I do not care. Her lovingly spun threads provide as comfortable a bed as ever I could wish for.

I am waiting for her return. I can see the light fading in the distance at the mouth of the cave. Night will be here soon and she will come to me. If I am fortunate she will bring me food and water. She will give me her love and her sweet medicine, which numbs my senses into unquestioning contentment. Until then I have no choice but to wait here, firmly attached to the network of threads she has so cleverly designed and created especially for me.

Sometimes I try to remember what my life was like before I was brought here. Was there such a time? Or have I always been here, kept safely under her watchful eye, at her beck and call. The life long gone is like a distant dream to me now. Yet I do remember there were once those who loved and cared for me; my family, I guess. Mother? Father? Sisters and brothers, perhaps? Though I cannot quite recall their faces, for when I close my eyes I can see no face but hers.

The longer she is away from me the clearer my memories become. I know I tried to escape once. She had not returned to me in the early evening as she usually did, and the clouds had fallen from my eyes. My mind somehow sharpened and I tried to cut myself loose from my bonds. I cannot believe my foolishness. Why would I want to leave? I have everything I could hope for and more than I could deserve. I am granted the honour of serving my beauteous one.

Even so, I have a memory that haunts me at these times, when she returns to me later than usual. A recollection of a dark forest, of bare running feet and the sound of something I greatly feared close behind me. If I concentrate hard I can remember branches whipping my face and the taste of blood in my mouth. I can feel the myriad of eyes fixed on my fleeing form. The creature gains pace on me with every step. My two legs, weakening with exhaustion, are no match for her many. I fall and there is a lightening-sharp pain in my ankle. I cannot rise. I shut my eyes tightly, not wishing to see the creature almost upon me. I remember nothing more.

As I wrestle with these images she returns and they fade instantly with the sight of her. The last rays of light paint sheen on her silky ink-black hair and flowing cloak. Her eyes shine at me from her white face like stars emerging from the darkness. She climbs up to me with ease. How is it that she can move so effortlessly across the threads whilst I remain helplessly glued to them? She climbs up over my body until her face is level with mine. I see a flash of delicate death-white skin and pointed razor-sharp teeth, and my focus is drawn to her almond eyes. She examines my eyes closely, her black pupils widen and I fear for a moment that they will consume me.

'So, my treasured one,' she whispers. 'Your mind is beginning to stir from its slumber. You must receive my medicine at once. I shall not return so late again.'

She lowers her head and I feel her soft ruby lips press against my throat. There is a flash of sharp pain and, for a fleeting moment, I feel an iciness shooting into my veins and my body shivers. I remember the fear I felt in the forest and the eight-legged shape towering above me. Both the shape and the fear subside quickly and are replaced with a benumbed adoration of my beloved lady.

'There you are, my prize,' she croons. 'I have restored you to perfection once more.'

She reaches into her robes and produces several pieces of fruit. In eagerness I try to pull my head forward to receive them, but my sticky bed holds me firmly. I must be patient until she is ready for me to eat. She sees my eagerness and smiles. She allows me to wait just long enough to know it is through her kindness alone that I am given the morsels, and then holds each piece before my mouth in the palm of her hand as my teeth tear hungrily at its flesh.

She stops before I have eaten my fill. My mouth remains open, like that of a baby bird pleading with its mother for more.

'That is enough for now. You must not become too strong or you may develop the will to betray me again, and I will not let that happen.'

She replaces the offering of food with the offering of her mouth. My hunger is usurped by my desire for my lady. Her tongue darts out and twists around mine. Her body smothers me. She prizes my lower half away from the web and winds her legs around me. She squeezes me so tightly that a wave of giddiness sweeps over me. I feel the power of her body, such strength that could snap me in two so easily should she wish it. I feel the completeness of her love.

She salivates. The glistening, silver liquid runs down my throat and over my eager breasts. I feel her hands gliding over them, rubbing in the moisture like ointment. Her hands slide down my body. My pelvis rises to meet them as they reach my sex and begin to massage the tender folds. All her limbs caress me. They wind around my body, covering me completely in her juices. I feel my own moisture burst into the wall of my vagina and I am soaked inside and out.

She mounts me again, and her body begins to writhe against mine. Flesh slides against flesh in slippery pleasure. The whole intricate network of threads sway with the motion. I am rocked in the cradle. She climbs higher, parting her velvet garments to press her protruding sex against my mouth. My hair is stuck firmly to the threads and my head cannot move, so I may use the skill of my tongue alone to please her. I slither it around her mound of flesh, covering every inch. I suck her into my mouth. She pushes herself further into me, lapping up the pleasure I give. She reaches down and releases each of my arms. I wrap them around her, caressing her curved body through her soft cloak and then reaching beneath its layers to the alabaster skin within. I run my hands over it, down her elegant spine and over the curves of her ass. I pull her closer to me, engulfing even more of her flesh. I feel her pleasure mount and hear her soft murmurs.

My hands press deeper into her flesh, the fingers of both pushing gently against her opening. Her flesh parts under their touch, sucking them inside as she shares with me the most private secrets of her body. I feel her form begin to change. Soft, silken hair grows on her legs as the two become eight. I am unafraid. I find her even more beautiful in this, her true form. Eight legs with which to embrace my every part. A multitude of eyes with which to keep me under careful watch. I am bursting with love for her.

She returns the pleasure I give her. Covered in her dew I am able to slide easy from my bed. She carries me down to the floor of the cave and begins to wind me in a cocoon of her thread. She spins around me so fast that I almost faint with dizziness. The sparkling strands are woven all over my body, filling every fold. They tickle me sensuously and I squirm within the cocoon, pressing my sex into the soft gauze and feeling it rub against me until I am jerking with pleasure. My arms are pulled tightly against my sides and my head covered in a mask of thread.

Finally her body emits a sturdy thread, hoisting me off the ground and I am left dangling and spinning, wrapped cosily in my bonds. I float all night in blissful senselessness, and above me, in her castle of thread, my lady gazes at her treasure.

# Two Women
## (the Submissive to the Suffragette)

*If you please, ma'am, who am I*
*That you should fight for me*
*Against 'male oppression' through the years*
*So women can be free*

*I know you strove to prove our worth*
*Great chance you had to take*
*Pray do not think I disregard*
*Your struggles for my sake*

*You clench your fist and stamp your feet*
*To see me serve and bow*
*And take such treatment from a man*
*That you would not allow*

*If you please, ma'am, calm your rage*
*Your gift I'll not ignore*
*'Twas choice you gave and choice I take*
*As slave to man once more*

*For the Taking*

# Her Majesty's Obsession

*Another trip into the past, this story was inspired by the many rumours surrounding the practices of Queen Catherine de Medici, wife of Henry II of France. It is said that the queen had a penchant for spanking and that she would use any excuse to get her hands on the ripe young bottoms of the servants and the ladies of her court. Countless times I have lain in bed wondering what life would have been like as a lady of the court, or perhaps one of her maids. How would it feel to be put over the knee of a queen and feel the royal hand descend against my flesh?*

*Here is my interpretation of life and games with the unorthodox lady. It is not based on evidence or historical accuracy, so I trust you will forgive any anachronisms and enjoy it the way it is intended, as a wishful fantasy.*

Her Majesty was coming. We could all hear the smart dig of her heel on the polished floor as she approached the chamber. The sound struck fear into our hearts but we could do nothing but stand and await her presence. The eight of us exchanged nervous glances. Quickly and efficiently we checked each other to make certain our garments were straight, that our hair was tidy and that our hands were spotlessly clean.

We shuffled into our places in the line. I, being the youngest and smallest, took my usual place at the end. I do not know why we made the effort. It would make no difference to our fate. The queen would find some reason to have her way with us.

The doors swung open and the queen burst into the room and greeted us, as she always did, with a wide smile.

'How are my sweet girls this morning?'

'Well, thank you, Your Majesty,' we chorused.

'I am glad to hear it,' she chimed. 'I hope you have all been on your very best behaviour since last we met.'

'Yes, Your Majesty.'

'Really? Well, we shall see.'

The line stiffened. We all stood as straight as we possibly could though we knew that, no matter what we did, fault would be found and consequences would follow. The queen wandered slowly around the first girl, who must have been almost six foot in height. I was always amazed at how the tiny figure of the queen could make such a large female quake with fear.

'You have not darned that hole in your apron,' the queen remarked.

'I-I am sorry, Your Highness,' the poor girl stammered. 'I simply have not had the time.'

'Well, fortune shines upon you, as I *do* have the time to remind you to do so. Turn around and raise your skirts.'

We had all learned very quickly that to protest merely resulted in a more severe punishment. The girl spun around, raised her skirts and screwed up her face in preparation for what was to come. She received ten hard slaps and swore she would attend to the hole the moment she was dismissed.

The second girl was slightly shorter in stature than the first, but ever so slight in build. She positively trembled as the queen's gaze turned to the unsightly stain on the hem of her dress. She received twice as many smacks as the first girl and was in floods of tears by the end. My heart bled for her and I wanted to yell for the queen to stop, but my fear silenced my thoughts.

The queen continued her morning inspection, determined that every single one of us should be sent about our duties with sore, ruby-red derrieres.

After what seemed like forever, she finished with the petite brunette beside me and it was my turn. Everyone in the room knew I was her favourite, and I was given all the honours that went with that privilege but also had to endure the price of her affection.

I had been extremely careful this morning. I had made certain that every seam was straight, every hair in place, every inch of my dress spotless and every inch of my shoes polished to perfection. The queen stared at me for a very long time, her brow creased. Inside I was in turmoil, but I remained rigidly at attention.

A smile broke on the queen's lips, and she reached out and gripped one of the hooks on my dress. It must have been loose, for with minimal effort it came away and tumbled to the floor.

'Her dress is missing a hook. Horse her!'

I stared at the hook in dismay as two of the girls got onto hands and knees beside each other on the floor. The rest laid me across them and hoisted my skirts to my waist.

'Hold her down, girls,' Her Highness commanded. 'We all know of her tendency to wriggle under the power of my palm.'

Their strong hands gripped my wrists and ankles firmly. The queen stood over me, rubbing her palms together in eagerness. Then the roasting began. The broad and relentless palm descended in a well-practiced flurry. The biting scorch set in immediately. My bottom felt as though it had been thrown to the mercy of a raging hornet's nest. I tried to kick but my legs were held fast. There was no escape from the queen's rampage. I twisted my body and shook my head fiercely.

'Be still!' snarled one of the servants beneath my ribs.

'Let me go,' I cried. 'It is not fair! My punishment is always worse than anyone else's no matter what I do.'

'Such disrespect!' announced the queen, and she took hold of a wad of my long hair and pulled it hard so that my head was forced back. I screamed and fought but every struggle made her pull tighter. She recommenced the spanking still clutching the hair tightly with her left hand. I do not know which hurt more, my head or my bottom, but the cunning trick served its purpose for my struggles ceased. I could do nothing but passively endure the punishment.

Eventually the queen seemed satisfied that I was nicely coloured and she allowed everyone to go about their duty. Her Majesty had been granted more than her share of irony, as she set me the task of tending to her poor overworked hand with ointment as she breakfasted.

Men were never permitted to attend the queen's little events. They were strictly for the prettiest of the court's ladies. At first I had wondered whether the proceedings were enjoyed by all or merely tolerated for the sake of remaining in the queen's favour. I had quickly come to the opinion that they had been in the company of the queen for so long her tastes had rubbed off on them and they were just as hungry for a quivering red bottom as she was. What was certain was that the ladies were all extremely careful not to be late.

I knew I should have been helping prepare the meal, but I simply could not bear the thought of all those horrid potatoes awaiting me. I had cut my finger every time I was given the task of slicing them and then I would feel the wooden spoon of the chef for my clumsiness. So I made myself scarce for most of the day, dashing here and there appearing to be busy with a range of tasks.

At four o'clock I was prompt to perform my duty in assisting the dressing of the queen. How I always marvelled over the delicate embroidery of her skirts and the glittering splendour of her jewellery as I fastened each item in place! Shyly, I also admired the creamy whiteness of Her Majesty's complexion.

She was impatient; the ladies would be here at any moment. At last she was ready and set me the task of carefully folding each of her previously worn garments and storing them neatly in her closet. This was no small task. The queen was immensely fond of clothing and generally wore layer upon layer of silk and lace.

As I worked I could hear the chatter and giggles of the ladies gathering downstairs. The menagerie of laughter grew. From time to time I would hear a shriek and knew exactly why it had occurred. As I lifted the final garment from the bed I noticed it had been placed over a small cake. I thought it odd. Perhaps the queen saved them in case she grew hungry during the night. Seeing the tasty morsel reminded me of how ravenous I was. I had been avoiding the kitchen all day and consequently missed out on the concession of stealing titbits from the chef's recipes. The cake looked so delicious that I simply could not resist it. I was certain the queen would not miss one little cake.

Had I not been so hungry I might have thought more

carefully about my actions. The moment I bit into it a strange taste filled my mouth. I pulled the rest of the cake away from my mouth and saw that the inside of it was bright blue. I raced to the mirror and poked out my tongue. Sure enough, the telltale dye had stained it a dark indigo. I knew then that I had fallen right into the queen's trap.

The door burst open and four of the servants seized me. The largest of them hoisted me over her shoulder.

'Help!' I shrieked. 'Why are you doing this?'

''Tis the order of the queen,' they replied.

I struggled so violently that they had to set me down. The large lady pushed me to the floor and sat her enormous bulk upon my chest so that I was almost smothered by the malleable flesh of her gigantic buttocks. But the act soon achieved its purpose, knocking the air and the fight out of me. She prised my mouth open and grabbed my tongue between her bloated fingers.

'Just as Her Majesty said!' she announced. 'You selfish little glutton!'

To my relief the lady stood up. She did not bother to lift me again but grabbed hold of my hair and pulled me the entire length of the hall and down the staircase thus, with the other three servants tottering along behind.

'Please, sisters, let me go,' I whimpered.

'It is your fate or ours. We shall feel a greater deal of her wrath if we let her little favourite escape.'

The four servants dragged me into the dining hall and deposited me in the middle of the polished floor.

'So, you were caught, were you?'

I glanced upward as I heard the queen's voice. The table was laid as if for a grand feast, with no less than twenty ladies of the court sitting around it, eyeing me curiously and suppressing giggles.

'Poke out your tongue, child.'

I had no choice but to obey.

'Just as I suspected,' the queen gloated. 'Ladies, I am certain you will be shocked to learn that this naughty girl you see before you has had the impudence to steal one of my cakes.'

The ladies shook their heads in feigned disapproval. The queen turned back to me.

'And how dare you present yourself to me in such a state?'

I realised the truth of her words. All the pins had fallen from my hair and it now fell about my shoulders as though I were a beast. I looked down to see that my dress had been ripped during the struggle and now the pink flesh of my breast pouted through the torn material. I tried to cover it with my hand but it was too late.

The queen advanced. She raised her voice to address the entire room but her eyes never left me for a second.

'This, my dear ladies, is the most badly behaved of all my maids. She has been here not two months, but I have had more trouble with her than the rest of my servants put together. And by a twist of fortune she also happens to have the most pleasing appearance as well.'

She stood directly over me.

'Well, stand up, girl. Where are your manners? Curtsey to the lovely ladies. It is the least you can do after humiliating me so. They must think I have no control over my servants, and we both know that is not true.' The poignancy of her speech was not wasted on me. I knew that, even now, her imagination was working on a wicked plan. So I promptly obeyed, performing one of my most elaborate curtseys for the ladies.

'Very good, my darling, now show the nice ladies how

pretty you are. And I can assure you, my friends, that her face is merely the beginning of her charms. She has a treasure far greater that is still hidden from your view… for the present moment.'

She turned and headed back to the table.

'Well, ladies, I shall leave her fate to you. What shall be done to punish this naughty miss for her outrageous behaviour?'

There was a bustle of excitement and whispers were passed around. I remained where I was, standing awkwardly before them in the centre of the room. Every now and again a head would turn to glance at me and then flick back again with a cunning smile. And all the while the queen simply watched me, relishing my discomfort.

'Ladies, your time is up, what delicious retribution have you decided upon?'

At a nod from the rest, one of the ladies stood and walked over to the queen. She bent down to whisper in Her Majesty's ear, and the queen let out a burst of laughter.

'Very well, my dears,' she beamed, 'it shall be done.'

She called over one of the servants and sent her scurrying out of the room, then the ladies stood and advanced on me like a pack of hungry wolves. Each grabbed hold of a section of my garments and pulled with all her might, and in no time my apron was in shreds and my dress shortly followed suit.

To my added horror they then began to pull at my undergarments, but the queen raised a hand to stop them.

'Patience, ladies. All in good time. Is it not better to first admire the gift in its wrapping before enjoying it? Come here, my dear.'

The gathering of ladies parted as I made my way slowly

towards the seated queen. She stood and wrapped her arms around my waist as I neared, and I could feel her hands gathering up my slip at the back to display the full moons of my buttocks.

'You see, ladies, the gracious Lord is fair. It appears he ensures that the naughtiest maidens are assigned the most beautiful of bottoms, thus making them so much more enjoyable to punish.'

I blushed with shame, knowing all too well that one or two marks remained on the area she now displayed from a scorching I had received earlier. Behind me the ladies fell over each other to view the presented area. The servant returned, and my eyes widened when I saw what she carried in her gloved hands – a bundle of long stems of stinging nettle!

The queen undid the button on my slip and pulled it to the floor, leaving me bare but for my torn undershirt reaching to my waist.

Each of the ladies scampered over and selected a nettle branch, then formed two straight lines about four feet apart stretching the whole length of the room. The queen took her place at the far end, between the two lines facing me. I gulped as I realised what they meant me to do. I had little time to think, however, as the queen bellowed.

'Let the punishment commence!'

I dropped to my hands and knees and began to crawl over the smooth surface of the floor. I reached the beginning of the procession of ladies and felt two whips of nettles slice through the air and land across my bottom, one torturing each buttock. I winced as the tiny needles jabbed my flesh. They stung so intensely that I stopped and put my hands to my bottom. I should have realised my foolishness. The whippy branches swung again depositing more searing pricks on my bottom and the hands that tried to protect it. I yelped and began to crawl as quickly as I could between the rows of whipping ladies.

As I passed each pair they did their best to add to the scorching. Some would swish the nettles down like a lash; others would brush them lightly over the round curves of the skin so that they pierced slowly and accurately. I could not scramble fast enough and I squealed with every unfortunate encounter. The ladies fell apart with amusement to see my bottom wriggling and jiggling to dodge the angry bites of the nettles and hear my cries of 'oh oh oh' when it could not.

At last I reached the end of the hall and endured the final lusty swipes, and then threw myself at the feet of Her Majesty in exhaustion.

'Well done, ladies,' she said. 'Now let me examine the result.'

The queen bid me stand. She spun me around and bent on one knee so that she had an excellent view of the torment the ladies had produced. Her elegant fingers grazed gently over the round, fleshy orbs before her. I whimpered at her touch, which seemed to ignite the sting even more. I turned my head and glanced down over my shoulder. My poor buttocks were dotted with hundreds of tiny red spots where the needles of the contemptible plants had pricked the tender skin.

'Hmmmm,' the queen contemplated. 'An adequate job by all parties, I do believe. However, the left side has been dealt with slightly more efficiency than the right side. I would therefore ask that all of the ladies on my left turn around, raise your skirts and offer you bottoms to the ladies on my right. Ladies, you may deliver one stroke only so be certain it does justice to your target.'

Then as the high-pitched caterwauls and giggles filled the room, the queen sauntered back to her throne at the end of the table. When all of the ladies had rejoined her there, half of them lowering themselves with utmost delicacy onto their chair cushions, the queen decided that I alone should serve the meal. I scurried over to collect my slip but the queen shook her head.

'Ah, ah, ah,' she admonished. 'As you are, if you please.'

I lowered my eyes and nodded and scampered as quickly as I could into the kitchen. Once out of the queen's sight my hands darted down to cover my dark triangle of hair and my crimson skin behind. I shut my ears to the laughter of the other servants.

'You will get yours soon enough,' I said, trying to retain an air of dignity. 'No one is safe from her clutches. You know that.'

I did my best to be careful, but there were so many ladies to serve and some of the dishes were so laden with delicacies that my slender wrists could barely lift them. Twice I stumbled. Once I even spilled a bowl full of steamed fruit onto the lap of one of the ladies and was promptly rewarded with several infuriated smacks. Some of the ladies took advantage of my proximity as I bent over to place the dishes in front of them, slipping their curious hands across my skin and darting them between my thighs. I dared not call out for fear of another beating.

When the last dish was in place I was made to stand facing away from the table with my hands upon my head like a schoolgirl, and my still-red bottom in full view. The ladies' stomachs feasted upon the delicacies and their eyes on me.

The delicious smell of the food teased my nostrils as they chattered about their most recent adventures and scandals. My arms began to ache. I shifted the weight from one foot to the other and back again, but still the ladies talked and ate. At last the knives and forks were set aside and the eaters commented that they had been naughty and devoured far more than they should have.

The topic turned again to the queen's favourite subject and what she saw as 'the only way to deal with disobedient maids'. I had hoped to be dismissed and that the queen would choose to turn her attention to another of the servants, but there was to be no such luck. Such was the downfall of being Her Majesty's favourite.

'For my own part,' remarked the queen, 'I do not care greatly for the implements of punishment. I refuse to surrender to any tool the pleasure of feeling the buttocks begin to warm directly beneath my palm. I will wager that I can make my little girl squeal just as loudly using nought but my own skin as you ladies with all your fine nettle whips.'

The queen patted her lap.

'Come to me, girl, you know what to do. You find yourself in this position far too often, do you not?'

I blushed and nodded. The ladies watched eagerly. I lowered myself as daintily as possible over her knee. I could feel the queen's delight. She was in her rightful place and I in mine. I sucked breath audibly as she rested her palm against the tender wounds. The ladies gathered round her, ready for the spectacle to begin.

'You have done an adequate job, ladies, but just watch what magic I can perform without the use of a wand.'

I did not yell out as the first spank landed, nor even the first few. The queen rarely began harshly, preferring to build the intensity of the punishment as it gathered speed. But by the fifteenth collision between her palm and my poor buttocks I was squawking like an infant. The juvenile position I was forced to adopt added to the humiliation. It stripped me of any last shreds of decorum I held to, especially as I knew that the rest of the servants would be observing the entertainment from behind the many doors and passageways.

At first I tried to keep my legs closed in order to protect my modesty, but now the sting in my nether regions was so intense that I kicked wildly and could not help presenting the engrossed women with a full view of the fleshy intimacies between.

'You see, ladies, I consider it my God-given duty to correct the behaviour of naughty girls. And I must admit that I derive a great satisfaction from performing my duty well.'

The spanking was thorough, and my howls left the ladies in no doubt of the effectiveness of the queen's methods. Her Majesty gave a few final tremendous wallops and then allowed me to stand again. I rubbed my burning bottom with vigour but nothing would lessen the smart. The ladies applauded enthusiastically as though they had just witnessed the most acclaimed theatrical event of the year.

'Now, as this young lady has detained us from our dessert, may I suggest she serve that as well? If you would care to assist me, ladies…'

Before I knew what was happening I found myself forced on my back across the centre of the table. Some of the ladies held me down while others collected strips from my torn dress and used the thick material to bind my hands above my head. Likewise my legs were pulled up over my head so that my body curled and only my shoulder blades rested on the table. My ankles were pulled wide apart and secured to the table legs.

The queen clapped her hands and the servants brought the desert dishes. They began to lay them on the table, but at a sharp word from the queen they arranged the contents of each dish on my body instead. Cake, jelly and cream smothered my skin and slid down to fill every intimate crevice. The coldness made me shudder and the sickly sweet smell filled my nostrils. Then on the queen's nod each of the ladies took a spoon and began to dive into the desert of her choice. The spoons tickled so much that I could not help giggling. My body squirmed so much that some of the food toppled onto the table and was quickly scooped up and squished into my intimacies once more. The queen relaxed back on her throne and watched the scene for a time, and then at last she stood.

'My dears, I will excuse you your table manners just this once. Cast away your spoons. There are some places that hands and tongues can reach far more effectively than spoons.'

And so the debauchery began. I closed my eyes and felt countless tongues at once swirling over my body. Some lapped at my toes, some traced up my thighs, some circled my nipples and some delved into deeper places. The tickling was merciless. I squirmed and shrieked in my bonds. Her Majesty, unable to resist the temptation any longer, called for the servants to remove her garments. The other ladies quickly followed her example and soon a pile of expensive dresses lay in one corner of the room.

The ladies clambered onto the table. A redhead with very large breasts grabbed a jug if cream and poured it all over the blonde hair of a squealing lady. The victim, dripping with cream, seized the culprit and turned her smartly over her knee. Cream dripped down and spattered everywhere as the screaming woman's generous ass was turned rosy-pink and her giant breasts bounced like balls on the table's shiny surface.

The scene excited the others. They dipped their hands in the sticky sweets and began to hurl and smear them over each other's curves. More desserts were sent for and this time the servants did not escape the excitement. The moment they arrived with the delicacies they were grabbed and dragged onto the table to join the fun. Before long every single one of us was covered head to foot in sticky mess. There was no determining who was queen and who was servant. Everywhere one looked food was being flung about as bottoms were slapped and licked. A chorus of moans filled the room.

Still bound tightly to the table, I watched the revelry progress before my very eyes. Everywhere I turned there was some unspeakably wicked act being carried out in full view. Bodies slid on bodies, forming a writhing sea. Tongues savoured and hands delved. Nearby five or six ladies were piled on top of each other and there was no distinguishing which part of anatomy was which. A lady next to me was poking cherries into every orifice she could find on her companion, and tittering as she tried to catch them in her mouth as they were shot from their hiding places.

Someone freed me from my bonds and flipped me over onto my stomach. The hands smoothed the cream into my back and bottom and pulled my lower half onto my knees. They pulled apart my slippery buttocks and a face was pressed deep between them whilst a greedy tongue penetrated deep into the tight hole there. Fingers slithered over my fleshy button, saturating it with goo. I gasped as the fingers worked to melt my shyness. I was pushed onto my back again and felt a soft body squash against mine. I looked up and saw a cream covered face above me. I recognised the blue, sparkling eyes of the queen.

'What a tasty morsel you make, my pretty one,' she cooed, and pressed her lips to mine. Our bodies slid against each other. She did not seem to care that I was lowborn. She was hungry for my body. We rolled over and over, our mouths pressed together as if we were attached thus. Others joined us and I felt dozens of hands all over my flesh. Someone's head was eagerly slurping between my legs. Two others were attending to my hard little nipples, and all the while the tongue of the queen danced intertwined with mine.

The ladies were merciless, and I could no longer resist the feeling that swept over me. I joined the rest of the chorus, screaming out my pleasure, my cries echoing around the enormous room.

It was almost two before I got to bed. Not permitted to use the proper bathing facilities, it had taken the rest of the servants and I almost an hour to get the stickiness out of our hair and our private parts.

As I lay there I realised I was no longer afraid of the queen. In fact, when I searched my heart I found nothing but love for her. I didn't even mind her spanking me any more. Of course it stung a little at the time, but the pain never lasted long and it made Her Majesty happy. Surely the pleasure of one's mistress was the sole duty of any servant. I faded into sleep with a smile on my lips, and dreamed of cakes.

*Restricted Pride*

# Emergence

*It may be the curse of a Christian upbringing, but there remains an element of guilt over any kind of expressed sexuality in many who have been raised as such. I believe that this is the reason I find the idea of sexual encounters with strangers so appealing. In this story I have decided to extend that idea to conjure a situation in which a girl never sees or knows anything about the Master who cares for and pleasures her. In the dark, when the obstacle of sight is removed, the restraints of guilt and embarrassment are loosened and one is free to indulge.*

*Inside her cocoon the worm waits*
*Relieved that her ugliness is hidden from view*
*But she holds a secret*
*A secret not yet ready for the world*
*About herself*
*About her feelings*
*They give her strength*
*Set her apart from the rest*
*For it is only when one has known ugliness*
*That one can begin to learn what beauty is*
*And be triumphant in it*
*Power is stripped from her body*
*Yet her soul grows stronger still*
*Soon she will emerge*
*And yell her secret to the world*
*'This is the way I am*

## And it is beautiful'

She heard the clock strike eleven. Her visitor would arrive soon. The thick curtains held back the moonlight and ensured the room was pitch black. She could see nothing. The bronze cuffs hugged so tightly against her skin that they were like fitted corsets. After all, they had been made especially for her. She had sat in patient silence as the smith wound his tape measure around her slender wrists and ankles, all the while attempting to catch her eye with a quizzical stare, but not once did she raise her eye line to meet his. She allowed him to perform his duty. Someone had paid him well to craft the objects and he had done so with great skill. They fitted like a second layer of skin over the first, and yet she had to strain hard against them before they would restrict her circulation, but now, in this relaxed position on her bed, she could barely feel them. They had become part of her, worn for twelve hours out of every day from eight in the evening until eight in the morning.

She knew nothing of her nightly visitor, he who had paid so richly to restrain her thus, arms and legs spread wide so that her body was fully stretched across the velvet bedclothes. His smell was all that told her he was a man. Beyond that she had only her imagination to endow him with face and form.

At first her head had been filled with curiosity. Why did he not let her see him? Was he disfigured? Or just shy? Eventually she abandoned the stream of questions for which there would be no answer. They no longer concerned her. She came to trust and rely upon what she knew; that he would be there and that he would give her pleasure.

During the daytime she was free to do as she pleased. The house itself was vast and its history dated back four centuries. She respected it for all its years and it pleased her to live there. Although she spent most of the daylight hours alone, she was never lonely. She had always shied from company anyway, and felt completely content. Her imagination had been a constant source of fun to her ever since she was a small child. Sometimes she would simply lie on the lawn at the front of the house and let the sun warm her clothes and her skin. Her mind would take her to a thousand places full of mystery and magic.

The day would pass and she would watch the sun descend on its journey behind the mountains and the sky turn purple in its wake. It was then that the ancient Japanese maidservant would emerge to fetch her from whatever task she was engaged in, and escort her to the room. The old woman never spoke to her. Perhaps she spoke no English. Perhaps she was mute. It didn't matter. Neither the woman nor the girl needed the use of words. Both knew her role and the routine.

The woman would take her to the marble bathroom and waited while she took off her clothes and climbed into the steaming bath. She would sit passively and obediently while the old woman scrubbed her thoroughly with a sea sponge, massaging the supple flesh beneath her crooked hands. The woman would then dry her with a thick towel and comb out her long dark hair until it glistened.

The woman would wait while the girl performed her ablutions; she would not get another chance until morning. When she was finally ready she would lie on her back on the antique pine bed. It had been placed in the centre of the room so as to be accessible from all sides. The woman's bony fingers would secure each cuff in place with the set of small silver keys. Then it was time for the mask. It appeared that her sightlessness was so important to her visitor that he did not even risk using a mere blindfold. The mask was made of soft, ebony leather. The scent of it was so strong at first it made the girl dizzy. It fitted across her entire face, leaving only two small holes for the nostrils. Its purpose could not have been to hide her features. She had always been a beauty. Fixed tightly over her mouth, it sealed her lips together so that she could not speak to him. Deprived in this way, her body became her eyes and her voice. It was her sole source of knowledge and communication.

Gradually she had learned to take comfort in the anonymity provided by the mask. She would think back to her old life. Beauty had been nothing but a curse. It had gained her the affection of an endless procession of lovers but she found she could not find contentment in any of them. They esteemed her as though she were a precious jewel. They filled her ears with praise, telling her over and over again how captivating she was. They would bring her orchids, her favourite flowers. They would take her to dine in the finest restaurants. They overindulged her every desire, but none had been capable of giving her what she truly wanted. How could they when she herself did not realise what it was?

She had tried to explain her feelings to one of her lovers, but his reaction had been fear rather than understanding. Defeated, she silenced her needs, never again daring to share her secret with the world.

In making her wear the mask, her visitor stripped her not only of her beauty but also of all the burdens and expectations that accompanied it. She was no longer something priceless that must be treated with respect and delicacy. There were those who, if they knew of her situation, would call her a prostitute. But even if that was so, she did not care. She found the concept noble. She took pride in being a vessel of pleasure and was happy that she produced happiness in another.

She had found it difficult at first to be restrained in this way, forced to be silent and still for so long, but over time she trained herself to relax her body. Now she could remain as unmoving as a statue for hours if needed, waiting patiently for her visitor to arrive.

She would startle slightly as she heard the creak of the door. She would turn her head in its direction, but more out of habit than from a hope to see him. She had decided long ago that, if it was his will to remain unseen, then this must be the way it was. The darkness made her feel warm and safe. It freed her imagination and her desire.

She could feel him draw near to her. She could feel the heat of his body and the smell of him filled her nostrils. The tingle of anticipation would run through her and begin to build. She would will his hands to her body, feeling she'd burst if she did not feel them but never doubting that she would.

She would wait for his touch, knowing it would come, but not from where. Sometimes she would feel him on her breasts, the sensation of fingers cupping them gently while a pliant tongue circled around the circumference of the nipples. At other times he would raise her waist, pushing a pillow under her back so as to gain access to her buttocks. He might trickle his fingers over them or pinch the skin lightly so that moisture filled her eyes. Sometimes she would feel him caress the soles of her feet, tickling her, though the mask stifled her laughter.

The caresses would work their way up past her ankles and knees to her soft thighs, her pleasure mounting with their ascent. She would spread her legs as far as she could but would only be chastened for her eagerness with more teasing.

Only when he was ready did he begin to centre his caresses between her legs. He would work on her with his tongue, readying her, dipping his fingers into her to feel her wetness. Unable to express her pleasure through her lips, her body would squirm and heave under his touch. He would remove his tongue and replace it with one of the phalluses. They all were smooth and flawless but differed in size. She suspected that they had also been fashioned out of bronze by the same smith that measured her for her cuffs. The metal was cold at first, making her flinch, but soon warmed to match her temperature. His tongue would return to her clitoris, doubling her pleasure. Her pelvis would move up and down, riding the instrument. He would loosen the chains around her ankles enough to allow her to bend her knees and elevate her sex. His fingers would rub the tender skin around her anus, beckoning it to open, and as soon as it did so it would be filled with one of the smaller phalluses. As the two shafts of metal penetrated her she would sometimes imagine she was being fucked by a machine, a mechanism designed and programmed for the sole purpose of female pleasure, a bronze lover without the handicap of emotion working tirelessly and efficiently towards that goal. She would lose herself in the fantasy as she drenched the metal with her orgasm. It was as though the whole universe melted around her and her body was the only thing to truly exist.

The restraints were effective. He had made certain of that. She could not have escaped his touches had she wanted to. Every evening he forced her juices from her and she felt no shame in giving them to him. There was none of the usual self-consciousness that comes with the aesthetics of the eye – none of the humiliation. The barrier of sight had been stripped away and the pleasure she felt was simple and guiltless. She was free to abandon herself to his gift and to her own imaginings.

Only when her ecstatic convulsions had died at last did he loosen the chains of her wrists and ankles and allow her to roll over onto her stomach before tightening them once more. He would wait patiently while she caught her breath and the strength flowed back into her limbs. He would remain silent and motionless as if simply absorbing her presence and revelling in the mastery over her. She was his and joyous to be so.

She would hear the creak of the leather as he unwound the whip, marking the beginning of the pleasure he sought for himself. She would never resist. Her pleasure came with a price and it was her duty to honour it. She knew it was only through her pain that he derived satisfaction. So how could she deny him? It was true that the pain was intense, but through that pain there burned a tremendous and defiant pride, as if she were showing the world the power of her endurance. She was certain that he saw her submission to the whip as a demonstration of her devotion to him. It is the meaning of pain that determines the experience of it. Her joy at showing her love made it bearable, even for her petite and slender frame.

Her body would brace itself, still flushed and ridden with perspiration. She would hear her old friend slice through the air and sting the curve of her buttocks. He administered it with surprising accuracy despite the darkness. So familiar was he with her position and every inch of her body's form that the use of the whip upon her had become almost instinctive.

The savage lash would lap at her unprotected skin, a lover planting scarlet kisses across the golden-hued flesh of her back and buttocks. She would remain perfectly still, burying her cries in the thick leather of the mask. The pain would rouse her flesh, reminding her that she was truly alive in this moment. It was as though it endowed her body with consciousness, as if it would call out, 'I am here. I exist'.

Her flood of tears stained the inside of the leather, carrying with them all her sufferance and joy. The pain gave her understanding. It endowed her with an identity and a purpose. It transformed her into an object of beauty. She smiled, knowing it was this she had been craving; simply to be at the mercy of the one she loved. She could not hate the sensation as long as it was he who created it. Her very blood obeyed him, rising to the surface under the summons of his lash. She would hear her visitor's growing exaltation, his breathing becoming heavier and more rapid though he never uttered a sound.

When he was ready he would cast the whip to the floor. She would feel his weight on the bed as he stood with feet on either side of her body. He would stride over her like a colossus and take his flesh in his own hands, and at last he would spray her naked skin with the hot, plentiful fluid of his love. The liquid was like precious lotion to soothe the fire in her wounds. She would twist and sway, allowing the blessed moisture to cover all the marks of the lash and dull the hurt.

Their nightly ritual complete, he would leave her to the darkness. She would relax her body once more, letting it sink into the velvet beneath. She would pull gently against her bronze cuffs and smile to feel them gripping her wrists and ankles. To her they were her visitor's arms locking her safely in a loving embrace until dawn. She wondered if she would be buried in them. She hoped so. At last she felt ready to share her secret with the world:

*'This is the way that I am
And it is beautiful'*

*The Summer Harvest*

# Virgin

*I am she whose secrets no man knows*
*I show them what they cannot have*
*Staying always on the periphery of their vision*
*Just out of their grasp*
*I am the untouchable*
*The queen of ice as yet unmelted*
*Purity in its true form*
*Unspoiled and unsoiled*
*Lain above the rest of man*
*By the unicorn's side*
*Its coat white as my soul*

*Then in one moment of one day*
*I will allow myself to be slain*
*And dragged back down to Earth for earthly pleasures*
*I will be speared as the hunter spears a fleeing doe*
*Passive after the kill*
*The sealed wound forced open to accommodate the staff*
*Rigid as steel*
*The union consummated once and only once*
*With eyes wide and round and bright as twin suns*
*Betrayed by my companion of snow*
*His determined horn piercing my flesh*
*What were two is one*
*As I consume him*
*The lock is snapped open by the key*
*And all the enigma of life revealed at last*

*Daydream*

# Afterword

I wanted to conclude this book by expressing my gratitude to you, the reader. Thank you for being brave enough to glance at something that much of society would not understand. I have poured my soul into the words and ideas within these pages and I am thrilled and deeply honoured.

I hope you have enjoyed your journey into my world. Perhaps you feel a little more enlightened about the mysteries that lie behind the eyes of young, submissive females, or perhaps you feel all the more perplexed. After all, fantasies, especially unusual ones, are complicated and highly subjective. Draw what conclusions you may but remember that these fantasies were captured by a single person at a single point in time.

I have gained enjoyment and fulfilment from writing this book. Each story and poem has enabled me to develop a more thorough understanding of my own sexuality. The ideas reflect my moods, experiences and imagination, and expressing them has helped me to begin life along the path of submission with excitement and pride. I hope my words have aroused and entertained you and that you will remember that, as you finish reading and put down this book, my own story is just beginning.

# More exciting titles available from Chimera

| | | |
|---|---|---|
| 1-901388-09-3* | Net Asset | *Pope* |
| 1-901388-18-2* | Hall of Infamy | *Virosa* |
| 1-901388-21-2* | Dr Casswell's Student | *Fisher* |
| 1-901388-28-X* | Assignment for Alison | *Pope* |
| 1-901388-39-5* | Susie Learns the Hard Way | *Quine* |
| 1-901388-42-5* | Sophie & the Circle of Slavery | *Culber* |
| 1-901388-41-7* | Bride of the Revolution | *Amber* |
| 1-901388-44-1* | Vesta – Painworld | *Pope* |
| 1-901388-45-X* | The Slaves of New York | *Hughes* |
| 1-901388-46-8* | Rough Justice | *Hastings* |
| 1-901388-47-6* | Perfect Slave Abroad | *Bell* |
| 1-901388-48-4* | Whip Hands | *Hazel* |
| 1-901388-50-6* | Slave of Darkness | *Lewis* |
| 1-901388-51-4* | Savage Bonds | *Beaufort* |
| 1-901388-52-2* | Darkest Fantasies | *Raines* |
| 1-901388-53-0* | Wages of Sin | *Benedict* |
| 1-901388-55-7* | Slave to Cabal | *McLachlan* |
| 1-901388-56-5* | Susie Follows Orders | *Quine* |
| 1-901388-57-3* | Forbidden Fantasies | *Gerrard* |
| 1-901388-58-1* | Chain Reaction | *Pope* |
| 1-901388-60-3* | Sister Murdock's House of Correction | *Angelo* |
| 1-901388-61-1* | Moonspawn | *McLachlan* |
| 1-901388-59-X* | The Bridle Path | *Eden* |
| 1-901388-62-X* | Ruled by the Rod | *Rawlings* |
| 1-901388-65-4* | The Collector | *Steel* |
| 1-901388-66-2* | Prisoners of Passion | *Dere* |
| 1-901388-67-0* | Sweet Submission | *Anderssen* |
| 1-901388-69-7* | Rachael's Training | *Ward* |
| 1-901388-71-9* | Learning to Crawl | *Argus* |
| 1-901388-36-0* | Out of Her Depth | *Challis* |
| 1-901388-68-9* | Moonslave | *McLachlan* |
| 1-901388-72-7* | Nordic Bound | *Morgan* |
| 1-901388-80-8* | Cauldron of Fear | *Pope* |
| 1-901388-73-5* | Managing Mrs Burton | *Aspen* |
| 1-901388-75-1* | Lucy | *Culber* |

| | | |
|---|---|---|
| 1-901388-77-8* | The Piano Teacher | *Elliot* |
| 1-901388-25-5* | Afghan Bound | *Morgan* |
| 1-901388-76-X* | Sinful Seduction | *Benedict* |
| 1-901388-70-0* | Babala's Correction | *Amber* |
| 1-901388-06-9* | Schooling Sylvia | *Beaufort* |
| 1-901388-78-6* | Thorns | *Scott* |
| 1-901388-79-4* | Indecent Intent | *Amber* |
| 1-903931-00-2* | Thorsday Night | *Pita* |
| 1-903931-01-0* | Teena Thyme | *Pope* |
| 1-903931-02-9* | Servants of the Cane | *Ashton* |
| 1-903931-03-7* | Forever Chained | *Beaufort* |
| 1-903931-04-5* | Captured by Charybdis | *McLachlan* |
| 1-903931-05-3* | In Service | *Challis* |
| 1-903931-06-1* | Bridled Lust | *Pope* |
| 1-903931-07-X* | Stolen Servant | *Grayson* |
| 1-903931-08-8* | Dr Casswell's Plaything | *Fisher* |
| 1-903931-09-6* | The Carrot and the Stick | *Vanner* |
| 1-903931-10-X* | Westbury | *Rawlings* |
| 1-903931-11-8* | The Devil's Surrogate | *Pope* |
| 1-903931-12-6* | School for Nurses | *Ellis* |
| 1-903931-13-4* | A Desirable Property | *Dere* |
| 1-903931-14-2* | The Nightclub | *Morley* |
| 1-903931-15-0* | Thyme II Thyme | *Pope* |
| 1-903931-16-9* | Miami Bound | *Morgan* |
| 1-903931-17-7* | The Confessional | *Darke* |
| 1-903931-18-5* | Arena of Shame | *Benedict* |
| 1-903931-19-3* | Eternal Bondage | *Pita* |
| 1-903931-20-7* | Enslaved by Charybdis | *McLachlan* |
| 1-903931-21-5* | Ruth Restrained | *Antarakis* |
| 1-903931-22-3* | Bound Over | *Shannon* |
| 1-903931-23-1* | The Games Master | *Ashton* |
| 1-903931-24-X | The Martinet | *Valentine* |
| 1-903931-25-8 | The Innocent | *Argus* |
| 1-903931-26-6 | Memoirs of a Courtesan | *Beaufort* |
| 1-903931-27-4 | Alice – Promise of Heaven. Promise of Hell | *Surreal* |
| 1-903931-28-2 | Beyond Charybdis | *McLachlan* |
| 1-903931-29-0 | To Her Master Born | *Pita* |
| 1-903931-30-4 | The Diaries of Syra Bond | *Bond* |

| | | |
|---|---|---|
| 1-903931-31-2 | Back in Service | *Challis* |
| 1-903931-32-0 | Teena – A House of Ill Repute | *Pope* |
| 1-903931-33-9 | Bouquet of Bamboo | *Steel* |
| 1-903931-34-7 | Susie Goes to the Devil | *Quine* |
| 1-903931-35-5 | The Greek Virgin | *Darke* |
| 1-903931-36-3 | Carnival of Dreams | *Scott* |
| 1-903931-37-1 | Elizabeth's Education | *Carpenter* |
| 1-903931-38-X | Punishment for Poppy | *Ortiz* |
| 1-903931-39-8 | Kissing Velvet | *Cage* |
| 1-903931-40-1 | Submission Therapy | *Cundell* |
| 1-903931-41-1 | Caralissa's Conquest | *Gabriel* |
| 1-903931-42-8 | Journey into Slavery | *Neville* |
| 1-903931-43-6 | Oubliette | *McLachlan* |
| 1-903931-44-3 | School Reunion | *Aspen* |
| 1-903931-45-2 | Owned and Owner | *Jacob* |
| 1-903931-46-0 | Under a Stern Reign | *Wilde* |
| 1-901388-15-8 | Captivation | *Fisher* |
| 1-903931-47-9 | Alice – Shadows of Perdition | *Surreal* |
| 1-903931-50-9 | Obliged to Bend | *Bradbury* |
| 1-903931-51-7 | Ruby and the Beast | *Ashton* |

\*\*\*

The full range of our wonderfully erotic titles are now available as downloadable e-books at our great new website:
**www.chimerabooks.co.uk**

Rosaleen has her own website at www.rosaleenyoung.com
and
Mike Crawley has a site at www.photofrenetic.com

All **Chimera** titles are available from your local bookshop or newsagent, or direct from our mail order department. Please send your order with your credit card details, a cheque or postal order (made payable to *Chimera Publishing Ltd*) to: **Chimera Publishing Ltd., Readers' Services, PO Box 152, Waterlooville, Hants, PO8 9FS**. Or call our **24 hour telephone/fax credit card hotline: +44 (0)23 92 646062** (Visa, Mastercard, Switch, JCB and Solo only).

**To order, send:** Title, author, ISBN number and price for each book ordered, your full name and address, cheque or postal order for the total amount, and include the following for postage and packing:
**UK and BFPO:** £1.00 for the first book, and 50p for each additional book to a maximum of £3.50.
**Overseas and Eire:** £2.00 for the first book, £1.00 for the second and 50p for each additional book.

*Titles £5.99. **All others (latest releases) £6.99**

For a copy of our free catalogue please write to:

**Chimera Publishing Ltd**
**Readers' Services**
**PO Box 152**
**Waterlooville**
**Hants**
**PO8 9FS**

or email us at:
**chimera@chimerabooks.co.uk**

or purchase from our range of superb titles at:
**www.chimerabooks.co.uk**

# Chimera Publishing Ltd

PO Box 152
Waterlooville
Hants
PO8 9FS

# www.chimerabooks.co.uk

chimera@chimerabooks.co.uk

\*\*\*

## Sales and Distribution in the USA and Canada

Client Distribution Services, Inc
193 Edwards Drive
Jackson
TN 38301
USA

\*\*\*

## Sales and Distribution in Australia

Dennis Jones & Associates Pty Ltd
19a Michellan Ct
Bayswater
Victoria
Australia 3153